T0277464

Sapelo Island

A Stella Bankwell Mystery

(THE SECOND IN THE SERIES)

Also by Ronda Rich

RONDA RICH

Sapelo Island

A Stella Bankwell Mystery

MERCER UNIVERSITY PRESS
Macon, Georgia

MUP/H1046

© 2024 Ronda Rich
Published by Mercer University Press
1501 Mercer University Drive
Macon, Georgia 31207

27 26 25 24 23   5 4 3 2 1

Books published by Mercer University Press are printed on acid-free paper that meets the requirements of the American National Standard for Information Sciences—Permanence of Paper for Printed Library Materials.

Printed and bound in CANADA.

This book is set in Adobe Garamond Pro / Georgia.

Cover/jacket design by Burt&Burt.

ISBN (Print)   978-0-88146-936-3
ISBN (eBook)   978-0-88146-937-0

Cataloging-in-Publication Data is available from the Library of Congress

*To Pat Hodnett Cooper, my sister-friend, who showed me an
insider's look at the beautiful Golden Isles.*

MERCER UNIVERSITY PRESS

Endowed by

TOM WATSON BROWN
and
THE WATSON-BROWN FOUNDATION, INC.

Sapelo Island

Prologue

CR

Ance McCoy looked at the clock again: 10:32 p.m. It had been a long, hard workday at the conference put on by his company—Malachi Pharmaceuticals—so they had all turned in earlier than the late nights they usually kept during these retreats. Most of the participants had left on the last ferry, but eight stayed behind for reasons unknown to them but which their boss had demanded.

Sapelo Island, off the coast of Georgia, straight across from the little town of Darien, was primitive in its beauty. Over 17,000 acres and twelve miles long, most of it is untouched by man, though there is a community called Hog Hammock, where descendants of former slaves, known as the Gullah Geechee, live and another portion of the island where wealthy people have built modest homes. The beauty of the island with thousands of Georgia pines, live oaks with moss hanging down, sandy roads and a beach of pure, splendid wonder, is a sight to behold. All the while, it is gloriously untouched by commercialism. It looks pretty much today as it looked when the good Lord made it all.

The crown jewel is the R.J. Reynolds, Jr.'s mansion, originally built by Thomas Spalding in the late 1700s, restored by Howard Coffin, the designer and cofounder of the Hudson Car company, then built to grander proportions by the scion of one of the wealthiest men in America.

R.J. Reynolds had built an empire from tobacco and Richard, his oldest son, did not squander his fortune though he didn't deny himself any pleasures including a yacht. He invested in aviation in the 1920s and helped to seed, as legend goes, both Delta and Eastern airlines. He bought Sapelo then took a genuine interest in marine biology, wildlife, and all of nature that made up the island plopped down in the Atlantic Ocean.

Ance punched his pillow in a bunch and laid his head, medium-brown color hair with many shades of silver, on the pile of goose down feathers. It had been Spencer Houghton's idea to come to the island. He had seen a documentary on a nature channel of some kind and when he realized he could rent the Reynolds home—called the Big House by the Gullah Geechee community—he decided immediately that it was the place for a corporate retreat. He was CEO and Chairman of Malachi so he could do anything he pleased.

The moon shined brightly through the thin curtains and Ance laid there, thinking of what history there might be in this big room. Who had set foot through its large double doors, looked out the floor-to-ceiling windows onto the fountains, or slept in this bed. It was certainly lumpy enough to have been slept in by many.

Zachary Smith Reynolds, Richard's brother, had died in their mansion in North Carolina, either by a self-inflicted gunshot wound or by murder, the trigger pulled by someone else. There had been much controversy about this because the Reynolds family insisted that he did not kill himself, yet they did not want to go through the publicity and personal torment of a grand jury or trial.

Why would he kill himself? Ance wondered, as he stared at the light blue ceiling. With this kind of wealth?

Spencer was the best friend to Ance who was the company's Chief Financial Officer. They always joked that they were closer than birth brothers because most brothers argued, other brothers carried deep resentment for his blood kin and, still, a few other sets of brothers downright hated each other. But Spence and Ance? They had never had a harsh word between them. Until tonight. Ance heaved a loud sigh, his heart as heavy as a fully-loaded cement truck.

In the not-dark-enough evening, he bent his arms under his head, propping it up and studied, in his mind, over the ugly little scene which, though not observed by others, had most certainly been heard. That was embarrassing because as the top two executives, they had agreed, many years earlier, to present a united front. As remarkably close friends, that deal had always been a cinch to keep. Until tonight.

Tonight's argument had broken a streak of which they had always been proud: they had proven that folks could be friends without disagreeing or, especially, being loud about it. Never once had either shown a sign of egotism. Until tonight.

Of course, whiskey had been involved. Too much of it. Right there, at that moment, in that ancient bedroom, Ance vowed he would never again take a sip of anything. Anyway, it tasted downright awful, drying out his tongue and burning like fire all the way from his throat to the bottom of his gut. He had no desire to try it again.

Ance, Malachi's brilliant CFO, reached over and turned on the lamp. He picked up an Erik Larsen book and read the same paragraph over and over. Aggravated, he laid down the book, opened the table drawer by the bed, and pulled out a Gideon Bible.

"Lord, let this open to a scripture I need." Ance could only shake his head and smile wryly when the book fell open to the third chapter of Malachi. He read it, starting at the verse that says, "Prove me now herewith, saith the LORD of Hosts, if I will not open you the windows of heaven, and pour you out a blessing, that there shall not be room enough to receive it."

Ance closed the book, thinking how much he had been blessed. Spencer Houghton was his best friend in the world. The two had gone toe-to-toe with a tremendous deal of tribulation the last several months. Together, they looked each problem directly in the eye and did not look away. Regardless of how fierce the battle might be, Spencer and Ance—the modern-day equivalent of the biblical David and Jonathan—could beat it. Though several of the problems had been staggeringly hard to wrestle away, nothing compared to a tax audit that had been going on for eighteen months. Ance, being

4

the CFO, was in charge of that hard-to-unscramble basket of broken eggs.

They both had barely been able to bear up under it. As Spencer climbed the corporate ladder of the company, founded by one of his great-grandfathers well over a hundred years ago, he took Ance with him. They were as thick as the mud that set at the edge of the Mississippi River. Spencer had only been graduated from Vanderbilt for less than two months when he met Ance. It was a bone-deep friendship that had carried them through wives, Ance's two children (one who was in constant trouble), and divorces. Spencer, who had married his college sweetheart, had never married again but he was considered a great catch—a nice-looking man with a face covered in kindness, sweet eyes and, thanks to the millions left to him by his aunt and, later, by his father, he was, by far, the wealthiest one in the Houghton family.

Ance suffered from restless legs and no medication ever helped so if he lay in bed too long, his legs began to tingle. Since he couldn't sleep, his legs hurt terribly. He crawled out of bed and picked up his bathrobe from the end of the bed having decided to take a walk through the house. He carefully descended the staircase then stopped in the front room where, under the low lighting, he took a long moment to look at a stately portrait of Richard Reynolds who appeared distinguished, dashing, and serious in his World War II Navel suit.

He studied it for quite some time, knowing that Reynolds had died in 1964 and that his widow had sold the island

and house to the state of Georgia. The enormous upkeep moved from Reynolds' bank account to the State's.

He chuckled to himself. "Buddy, you died at the right time. You were able to enjoy greatly the spoils of your stock and dividends. But you should see what's happened since then. Legislation has regulated tobacco sales to the point that you might not be able to pay the light bill here with a quarterly dividend check." He shook his head as he thought: the tobacco industry would never return to its once-robust cash flow.

His head aching from the over-imbibing of the strong whiskey, he decided he was thirsty and wanted a glass of ginger ale that would also settle his stomach. He moved from the fireplace, above where the expensive portrait hung, and onward to the kitchen. Just as he flipped on the light at the doorway near Richard's portrait, he saw Mrs. Graham, the housekeeper who lived in Darien and who, normally, took the ferry back and forth but was staying in the maid's room while the Malachi group was there. In bed slippers, she was shuffling toward the open door to basement. Most probably, she was going to close it and turn out the light. The kitchen was softly lighted by a fluorescent, oblong bulb over the sink.

He saw her eyes widen in what appeared to be fear. Her hand flew to her mouth, then she screamed. Not loud but more like a stifled gasp that came from the back of her throat. She started to shake violently. Figuring it was a snake or mice, Ance rushed over to comfort her and handle whatever the problem was. When he looked down the stairs, what he saw would haunt him for the rest of his years to come. In one second, his heart was broken beyond anything he could ever imagine.

There, at the foot of the stairs, in a heap of death, was his best, most beloved friend. Spencer Houghton, the heir to hundreds of millions of dollars, was gone from Ance's life and gone from this earth.

How could this have happened? Then, the horrible thought came to him: had he, Ance McCoy, committed murder in an alcoholic haze of anger and unreasonable fury?

Then, just like Mrs. Graham, he began to shake violently.

Chapter One

℃℞

The old-fashioned Big Ben pewter clock with the two clanging bells and luminated numbers started to jingle and dance around on the nightstand next to Stella's bed. For $15, she had bought a clock that brought aggravation every time it rang so loudly. But she adored it because it was similar to one that had set beside her parents' bed in her old home place in her beloved mountains.

This was part of her new life since she had escaped her marriage from the recently-imprisoned Asher Bankwell and the Ansley Park mansion in Atlanta's prettiest part of town. When once she was the privileged wife of a man descended from old Atlanta money, he always encouraged her to sleep late.

"Stella, it is what wealthy women do in Atlanta. The more money you have, the later your wife sleeps," Asher used to say.

His mother, Miss Caroline, usually rang for her housekeeper to bring her breakfast on a tray of silver and fine china, around 10:30. Then, she leisurely read the Atlanta newspaper, scanned the *Wall Street Journal*, read a bit of whatever book she was reading then, close to noon, she slipped out of her luxurious bed and dressed as if she were going out. She was usually in a simple dress but sometimes she wore slacks, a shirt, cardigan and a pair of Tods loafers. Everything she owned was expensive. Often, though, she never saw a person except her service staff of housekeeper, cook, gardener, driver and pool man. But it made her feel good about herself and allowed her to pretend that life was like it used to be thirty years ago when every person in Atlanta society conducted themself as she did. She certainly did not approve of the young generation who increasingly wore no make-up and too many young women who often sported a sloppy ponytail or covered their hair completely with a baseball cap.

If she happened to have a luncheon, a charity event or other tiresome appointment with an accountant or McCager Burnett, her estate attorney, she reluctantly pulled herself from bed earlier and adorned herself in a designer dress, with two-inch heels for the meeting. Always, she carried a black Launer bag, just like the ones England's Queen Elizabeth had loved. It was reasonable for the woman who considered herself the queen of Atlanta society to dress like one.

Asher wanted Stella to carbon copy his mother but Stella, a simple girl from the Appalachian foothills, had resisted because it never felt comfortable or familiar to her. In fact, it made her feel guilty when she thought of her childhood when her father, Sims, and her mother, Martha Annie, arose at the break of dawn each morning for a hot, hearty breakfast guaranteed to see them through a long day of hard work until supper on the farm at Turner's Corner, about 80 miles north of Atlanta yet a world away from Wedgewood china, Lalique crystal, and antique pieces crafted during the late 1700s. That was Asher's world. Not hers.

Usually, now in her new fancy life, she had arisen no later than nine, slipped on her robe and had a simple breakfast at the kitchen table with their housekeeper, Lana (affectionately known as Lana Banana) as they talked about the things that close friends discuss like Lana's sister who, she claimed, was a hypochondriac.

"Miss Stella, it every day she sick," Lana complained. Still fairly new to the English language, she often left words out of her sentences. "I tell her, 'When you really sick, how we know?'"

And, almost always, they talked about Neely, Stella's stepson who had turned from a precious, loving child into a raging terror. Both women were heartsick about his ugliness and disrespect as a teenager. Now, he, too, was in a federal prison—his misfortune was that he had just turned the legal age of eighteen—without bail as both he and his father awaited the trials that would, most likely, put them in prison for years to come. It seemed, at least in Atlanta, the rich were sentenced more severely. And probably rightly so. They had money so why make more dollars illegally? Stella, US Marshal Jack "Pepper" Culpepper, former governor McCager Burnett and Chatham Balsam Colquitt IV, aka adorable but sometimes exasperating Chatty, had busted Asher and his lover, Annabelle Honeycutt, at the McKinnon Airport on St. Simons Island over a money laundering scheme.

Annabelle. What a piece of work. But that's a story for another day.

"Justice always comes to those on this earth who wear designer dresses without underwear," Chatty had proclaimed. "I'm pretty certain that's what the Bible says."

"No, Chatty," replied Stella, his best friend in all the world, who was staying in his guest house for a few days after the criminals had been tucked into nice, steel beds with thin mattresses. The Colquitt mansion was a stone's throw from the Governor's mansion in the toniest section of Atlanta. She had walked across the perfectly manicured lawn with pristine hedges and passed Chatty's adored hydrangea bushes to have dinner with him. She had returned to Atlanta to pick up some personal items from her old Ansley Park House which the federal agents—thanks to the intervention of Marshal Jackson Culpepper—had agreed she could retrieve. Of course, an agent was assigned to follow her through the house, but the truth was that the federal agents were grateful to her because, in bringing down an international ring of embezzling and money laundering, she had made them all look good.

"I don't recall ever reading that in the Old Testament or the New Testament. And, when I was growing up at Turner's Corner, we never missed church at Mt. Pisgah. I received perfect attendance pins for Sunday School twelve years in a row. Not to mention all the Vacation Bible Schools I attended." Here, she had stopped and laughed. "One time, we had boloney sandwiches with white bread and lots of mayonnaise. I was around nine years old and I think I ate seven sandwiches. No one said anything. They just let me make a pig of myself."

Chatty, the scion of old money and trust funds that would carry him extravagantly to heaven, (Chatty had, recently, begun to worry that heaven was sure to be a letdown from the life he had on earth) always had a retort.

"I do not believe I would tell that, were I you. It's unseemly. And who, of any breeding, eats boloney or rather bologna as it is properly known." He shuddered and his well-fed belly jiggled.

"Chatham," Stella was serious when she called him by his Christian name, "you forget that I don't have breeding. I'm not a dog or even a white-faced Hereford like my daddy used to stock on the farm. I have mountain raising and we often enjoyed, many times, a fried boloney sandwich with Duke's mayonnaise. My daddy was particularly fond of fried Spam sandwiches. Or sometimes he put the Spam on one of Mama's homemade biscuits."

Chatty's face turned green and he looked like he might give up the caviar and crackers that he had just devoured, doused fittingly with two glasses of Dom Perignon champagne.

"That is the most uncivilized thing I have ever heard. Spam? Wasn't that for South Pacific natives or third world countries where people got donated food from more sophisticated countries?"

"There is so much about life you don't know," Stella replied with a shake of her head. "Few people can afford caviar and Dom Perignon."

He took a sip from a fine crystal champagne coupe, the antique kind, not the flutes that people now use. The glass was paper thin. You could almost break it off with your finger. Chatham Balsam Colquitt IV possessed only the finest crystal, china, and silver ever made. Some of it was well over a hundred years old and several pieces were closer to 200 years old. One piece of silver, he grandly proclaimed, had been hand-crafted by Paul Revere.

"Really? I am not acquainted with any such people." He took a sip of champagne and contemplated on it for a bit then commented with counterfeit sympathy. "My heart goes out to them. I will ask my bingo class at church to pray for them." He thought for a second, characteristically placing a large hand to his chin, then said, "Or do you think the prayers of gamblers in the church hall are heard by the Almighty?"

Stella, for nine years, had known the life of an Atlanta socialite and was touted for her pleasing beauty and the old family money into which she had married. She had actually married the devil, but she didn't know it then. She had lived in grand style with designer clothes and many jewels. In fact, one year, she had purchased so much Chanel that she was invited to the Chanel fashion show in Paris and placed on the front row. This, incidentally, was a trip that Chatty happily joined, proclaiming, "It is improper for a woman who

13

represents a family of stature to travel alone to a foreign country, not even one as fine as the grand old city of Paris.

No more.

Thanks to the trio of criminals—Asher, Annabelle and Neely—Stella was now living a simple, fairly uncomplicated life on St. Simons Island, off the beautiful coast of Georgia. The cozy little cottage was painted in blue and yellow and had a kitchen so old that there was no dishwasher. But she didn't mind at all. She had made it her own with touches of bright pillows on the royal blue velvet sofa and she had splurged on some whimsical kitchen pieces from MacKenzie-Childs including a utensils holder, a set of cannisters, and her favorite—a whistling tea kettle—all in a black and white checkered pattern. It looked wonderful with the yellow cabinets accented with blue. There, too, she had added cheerfully colored towels and replaced the white plates with colorful pottery in orange, yellow, red and green. The sweet cottage belonged to the family of her childhood friend, Marlo Sloan. In return for their generosity, she helped out in the office of their booming real estate business.

"Well, if you can't live in Ansley Park or on Sea Island, I suppose you have done the best you can with this ancient relic," Chatty had commented, lifting an eyebrow as he looked around at Stella's decoration. He split his time between Atlanta's Buckhead and a house on Sea Island that was stately, bought by his parents in 1960 and updated by Chatty at least two times since he, an only child after his sister died of the red measles at age four, inherited it over 25 years ago.

Tragically, both of Chatty's parents had been killed in a private plane accident flying back from the Belmont Stakes where they had sat with the Whitneys in their box and Chatty's father had won a thousand dollars by betting on the winning horse. They left Chatty more money than he could ever spend and so much real estate that he often forgot what he owned and had to be reminded by his lawyer, McCager Burnett, a former Congressman and Georgia Governor.

"Thank you, Chatty," Stella replied with a sarcastic tone. "You're always such an encourager."

He smiled sweetly, the smile that always melted Stella's heart and took the edge off of any aggravation she felt for him. "I must say that you do have quite a touch with decorating. Perhaps you should consider interior design. I think you'd be marvelous. Do you know Elizabeth Pipe? She does all the homes on Sea Island. Perhaps she'd take you as a protégé. I think you'd do pleasing work for her."

That was Chatty: criticism in one hand followed by at least two compliments in the other hand. Yet Stella knew, just like former Governor McCager Burnett and his precious wife, Alva, always said, that Chatty loved her more than any person on the earth. He had proven it over and over, particularly, since all the ugliness had started with Asher and her divorce.

Thanks to Miss Caroline who, at the urging of McCager, had set up a sufficient trust for her, Stella could enjoy life while she unraveled the mess formerly known as her unflawed life. Cage, or Cager as he was known by those most familiar with him, except for Stella and Chatty, who always respectfully addressed him as Governor though he had not held political office in several years. Protocol was still observed by those of Southern aristocracy and those taught to be aristocratic as Chatty was continuing to teach Stella.

The loud, rattling clock continued to ring while Spigot, Stella's rescue dog—well, it's hard to say who rescued who—nudged Stella's perfect porcelain cheek. Spigot was always terribly annoyed by the obnoxious ringing.

Her velvety green eyes still shut, she blindly felt around the nightstand, grabbed the clanging aggravation, then shut it off from the back. Spigot laid her chin on Stella's arm and looked at her with complete adoration. Stella opened one eye and, seeing such sweetness, smiled while stroking Spigot's head.

"Okay, girl, I get the message," Stella mumbled softly. The sun was just beginning to rise as she pushed open the curtains. "Let me splash water on my face and I'll let you out."

Stella pulled the bright pink elastic band from her golden red hair, shook it out and shivered from the introduction of her bare feet to the cold, wide, heart of pine floors. The last two weeks had been chilly on St. Simons, yet the first two weeks of March had been delightful and indicative of why the once-isolated island had become packed with houses squished together.

ℭℛ

"It must have been a false spring," Stella had commented to Chatty over dinner at the King and Prince the previous night.

"False spring? I saw nothing false about it," He retorted.

"Chatty," she replied in the tone she used when she was trying to bring him down a notch or two, "it's a term we use in the mountains when it seems that spring has come but then we have a rude awakening because blackberry winter presents itself." She shivered at the thought.

"What in the tarnation—as Cager Burnett would say— is blackberry winter? My goodness, all these terms that you hillbillies use is nothing short of bewildering."

Stella didn't mind 'a'tall' as her people would say, that Chatty called her and her people hillbillies from time to time. The unfortunate fact—or fate, in reality—was that the city folks had discovered the beautiful mountains and were start- ing to build grand homes and cabins there. Many could hardly understand the Appalachian natives as they spoke. Some of the outsiders appreciated it and enjoyed the lan- guage. It was, after all, a child of Shakespeare's words and phrases. Others looked imperially down their noses and made unbecoming, unkind remarks. Stella rather liked being sin- gled out as a hillbilly, an original. And, besides, Chatty wasn't being unkind when he said it. At least, not to Stella's think- ing.

"It's a very cold spell that comes after the wild blackberry bushes have sprung forth with sweet, white blooms on them. The bitter cold knocks the bloom off the bushes and when the warmth returns, the berries grow."

Chatty looked at her skeptically. "Stellie, I love you. This you know. But, honestly, do you make this stuff up? If you do, you should write a book. Fiction."

Stella didn't hear him. She laid her head against the tall, upholstered chair in which she sat and let her mind wander back to the time on her family farm when the berries grew at the same time that the honeysuckle bloomed and the gorgeous fragrance that filled the air. Still, to this day, her Mama would walk out on the back porch, the screen door banging behind her, and take a moment to deeply inhale the sweetness of nature.

And, almost, without fail, she would say, "The Lord giveth us many beautiful things but honeysuckle vines and magnolia blossoms are two of my favorite."

In the gloaming of the day as the sun disappeared behind Blood Mountain—named for the vicious war over 200 years previous when two battling tribes had fought so bitterly for such a length of time that blood ran down the mountain—Martha Annie, Stella's Mama, would sit on the west side of the porch to watch the sun slip quietly away while enjoying the smell of the honeysuckle.

"Helllloooo!" Chatty said, bursting through Stella's daydream. "Are you still with us, Stella Bankwell? Or am I eating this delicious sea bass all alone?"

Stella smiled sweetly and sat up. Despite the havoc of the last fourteen months and, quite frankly, it felt like she had been cast among Satan's chief operation officers, she still retained the beauty that was so startling that strangers often stared from across a room or did a double take as they passed her. She threw her fetchingly golden-red hair back over her shoulders. She never noticed any of the admirers.

"Oh, I was just thinking of the soothing effects of home and how comforting it was."

Chatty threw his hands up. "Oh, glory to my soul! Stella, have you lost your mind? You grew up in a cow pasture with little varmints running around like possums and raccoons and armadillos. What is to miss about that?"

Chatty, of course, had grown up in the mansion he still lived in, a second home on Sea Island, and a 200-acre plantation just south of Savannah. He knew leisure. Stella knew pleasure.

She had long ago stopped being annoyed with such comments, unless she happened to be in a rare, bad mood.

"First of all, there were no armadillos and, secondly, we say 'varmits' not 'varmints.'"

"You also say 'drekkly' not 'directly' so, please, let's not begin on your mispronunciation of the English language."

Stella took a bite of her salmon and chewed slowly before swallowing, then commented, "John Benchley said to me the other day that he read that there remains a group of people so isolated in the deep part of the Appalachians that they still speak perfect King's language. As in King Edward VII, son of Queen Victoria. Isn't that amazing?"

"Okay, enough of this hillbilly talk. Tell me what you and the most dashing US Marshal are up to?"

"Who?" Stella asked innocently. "Jack Culpepper?"

Chatty rolled his eyes. "Yes. I prefer to call him Pepper because it fits him so well." Chatty winked. "He's spicy. Like table pepper. I know you think so because I see it in your eyes every time you see him."

It was possibly the truth, but Stella was not about to admit it to the biggest gossip in the state of Georgia. Other than Mona Windsor, that is.

ﻬ

It had only been two days since Chatty's birthday party at the Burnetts'. Stella and Pepper had developed a crush on each other during the time they were trying to unravel the criminal mess created by her husband, Asher, and his girlfriend, Annabelle. Thanks to Cager Burnett, Stella could now call Asher her "ex-husband." It takes 30 days to get a divorce in the state of Georgia. However, Cage, the crafty lawyer who had the clout of a former Congressman and Governor, threw some weight around and, quietly, got it done in 23 days. Of course, with over 100 federal indictments against Asher and that vixen, Annabelle, it had been fairly easy to do. There wasn't a judge in Fulton, Cobb or DeKalb Counties from whom Asher had not stolen so recusal was useless and, besides, Asher's attorney agreed, hopeful that it might soften Stella when time came for her testimony. It was possible. Stella was well known for her tender heart and sweetness. Except for that night at the Buckhead Country Club when she had acted out a bit too much. Still, Tim Casper, who was sitting lead chair in Asher's defense, had heard his mother and wife talk about it for days.

"What woman wouldn't do something like that and take on that floozy, Annabelle Honeycutt? I'm seventy-six years old and I'd've been glad to give it a go," declared Mrs. Casper, who lived next door to her son in Marietta, so close to the Atlanta Braves Stadium that they could sometimes hear the crowds cheer if one of the Braves hit a grand slam.

"Mama Casper, I'm with you. Stella showed much more restraint than I have in my little finger," Tim's wife, Jillian, agreed. Then, the two women discussed how much more they would have done.

When Casper got the call to represent Asher as well as set up a trust fund for Stella, he remembered those conversations very well. Of course, he would not have been able to sit first or even second chair, he would be third chair because of "conflict of interest." "Note to self," he said aloud. "Stock the jury with men." Of course, he knew that was impossible, but he'd certainly advise his co-council to keep the number of women jurors down as much as possible. Women could be meaner and harder to forgive than any man. Men tend to have short memories. Women? Longgggg. At a partners' meeting, he said, "I have faith in Stella Bankwell. She will be honest and forthright, and she won't try to cut him up into little pieces. She will demonstrate grace and I'm willing to bet that she throws in some forgiveness. She's better off now than she was."

This current mystery started on March 12th, the date that, as Chatty liked to say repeatedly, "The Almighty decided to bless this world with Chatham Balsam Colquitt IV and, just like that, the world became a better place."

To celebrate this remarkable birth, second in Chatty's eyes "to that precious wonder of a baby born in Bethlehem and, sadly, in a stable with donkeys and hay, I always have a big party. Jesus deserved much better. Happily, I was born at Piedmont Hospital, Atlanta's most prestigious hospital. Mother took me home from the hospital in a glorious outfit made by Queen Elizabeth's seamstress who had sewn all of her children's baby garments. Father knew the American Ambassador to Britian, and he arranged it."

There was always some kind of grand story like this that Chatty had to share. Those who did not know him well, thought he was a prevaricator but those like the Burnetts, who had been close to his parents and known him since he first graced the Piedmont nursery, knew it all to be true.

Gathered at the Burnetts' home on the anniversary of His Royal Highness, Sir Chatham's birth, had been a small group of friends including Edward Armstrong, who had designed the fabulous floral arrangements; Bess and Shannon Thompson; Pat Cooper and her daughter Kelly with her husband, Robbie, as well as Pat's son, Luke; Frankie and Gordon Strother and Valerie Hepburn, once President of the local college, who had stopped by for a quick drink because she was meeting her husband for a prior engagement.

Two weeks earlier, the Burnetts had thrown a big party at the Cloister on Sea Island to celebrate the bringing down of Asher and Annabelle's elaborate schemes that had simply scandalized Atlanta society. Chatty, surprisingly, had played a major part in Asher's undoing, the two of them having known each other since before pre-school. Ever since, Chatty had strutted around town, enjoying his celebrity and quick to remind anyone who dare to forget of his tremendous bravery and how he had shot one of the bad guys in the upper leg.

"First time, I ever held a gun. First time, I ever pulled a trigger. And look what happened? I saved the day! The FBI could really use a good marksman like me." Here, he would always push out his chest and toss back his head covered with a mane of dark brown hair mingled with strands of silver. Chatty had convinced himself—and many around him— that a hero's medal was soon to be awarded to him by the President himself, on behalf of the FBI and the US Marshals.

That night of the celebration of Chatty's entry into life, while the group mingled and talked, Pepper pulled Stella out on the enormous veranda that was separated from Chatty's house by a large hedge. Stella, though she hated to admit it to herself, was quite taken by Pepper and, as for Pepper, no one quite knew how he felt. But that night, THAT night in the cool air of the early spring, he had taken off his jacket, placed it around her shoulders, and then the moment came, the moment that every woman who has a crush on a man, wants to happen. They stood silently, his hands on her shoulders, he pulled her toward him as he stepped closer. Stella felt "swimmy headed" as her Mama liked to say. Her velvety green eyes looked into Pepper's marble blue eyes for a few seconds, then he leaned down to kiss her. But before his lips could touch hers, Mrs. Puckett, the Burnetts' longtime, much beloved housekeeper, stepped through the tall French doors.

Worry edging on panic clouded her plump, rosy-red cheeks. She always wore her silver hair in a neat bun but, on this occasion, strands fell around her face as though she had been running her fingers through it. Mostly her eyes were hazel, but they had the interesting feature of one being greener than the other that was mixed with green and blue. Fear leapt from those eyes.

She explained, in a high-pitched voice, that there had been a murder on nearby Sapelo Island and that her nephew, a day worker, who took the ferry to work each morning and then home at 4:30 p.m., had been arrested. He had decided to tent on the island for a couple of nights during the somewhat pleasant weather.

"Please, please, help him," she begged. "He is a good boy. A good, Christian boy. He goes to church every Sunday and he helps with the Sunday School Class for the ten- to twelve-year-olds. He would never do this."

And that is how a long-desired kiss was forgotten and Pepper and Stella found themselves with a new mystery.

Chapter Two

CR

Chatty watched Stella savor her last bite of salmon, then swallow it, followed by a dainty sip of water. He had just told her that he knew that she found Jackson Culpepper to be spicy, a remark that made her merely roll her eyes, when Stella felt a hand on her shoulder and Chatty jerked his head back, his eyes widened.

"Am I too late to join two of my favorite people for dessert?"

Stella felt a swirl of excitement in the center of her stomach and her heart flutter.

Chatty grinned big. "Well, lawd be," he said, using language he had learned from his nanny and loved to use for comical effect from time to time. "We were just talkin' about you, Marshal Culpepper."

Stella was speechless, wishing she had finished dinner earlier so she could reapply her lipstick. Never fear. Chatty was there to carry on.

"Do, please, my fine sir, pull out a chair and join us."

"Thank you," Pepper replied but not before he had glanced at Stella and given her a smile which melted her completely. "Stella, you're looking beautiful, as always."

Chatty just couldn't hold his tongue. Just could not do it. That moment would have been the perfect time to let the romanticism hang in the air as the moss hung in the trees but, instead, he had to add smog. "Beautiful, Stella. Did you hear that? *Beautiful*. Most men say 'lovely' never 'beautiful'. Or rarely. Even when I was in love with Cornelia Vangriffin who Asher meanly stole from me after we had been dating for two full moons, going on three." Here, Chatty lowered his tone which he always did when he was about to tell a secret or brag about an aristocratic connection. "She comes from the family tree of *THE* Vanderbilts. I think a Vanderbilt married a Vangriffin. There were so many "Vans" that I can't keep it all straight. It's a twig, maybe even a limb, but the Vangriffins are on the Vanderbilt family tree. All aristocracy and NO hillbillies."

Chatty didn't even stop as he said it, so used had he become to those little comments about Stella's roots. But he did adore Martha Annie, her mother, and everyone else he had met when he insisted, once, on attending a family reunion near the top of the mountain at Vogel State Park. Most of the time—MOST—Stella found his comments amusing. She long ago realized that the comments came from a place of hurt. Chatham had no immediate family left so, despite his great wealth and life of adventure, Stella had something he envied deeply: family, traditions, loving memories and reunions. She shared years of history with people, going back to the cradle. When you find the point of a person's pain, you understand what defines them. That was another Sims

Jackson lesson. Stella's daddy was born with the gift of wisdom. "Anyway, remember the one whom he asked to the junior prom because he knew I was going to ask her—Julia Brandenberry?"

Chatty took a breath because it was necessary to grab some air. In his customary gesture, he threw a large palm to his cheek and glanced out the window to the unusually rough waves hitting the beach. "You know, come to think about it, it is quite possible that Asher Bankwell is why I'm a proclaimed bachelor. He soured me on the dating process. That and I don't want a wife throwing away my hard-earned money."

Here was her chance and Stella grabbed it. "Hard-earned money? You've never worked a second in your life."

He put his hands on the table and moved closer. "Yes, Stella, that is quite correct. But someone did. In fact, as much money as I have from both families, there were more than several who worked hard." He took his enormous hand, with a large family crest ring adorned in gold and rubies on his fourth finger, and placed it on his heart over his light blue seersucker jacket. Dramatically, he closed his eyes, dropped his head and said, as though he was Lawrence Olivier of the 1930s theater, "May they all rest in peace, sweet peace, as wrought to them by angels."

Pepper threw back his head, exposing his gorgeous profile, and laughed heartily. He liked Chatty, as annoying as he could be in not allowing him time with Stella, and enjoyed the amusement that always trailed along with him. Chatty's person was swallowed up in a mist of comical comments and clever insights. The delivery was often as funny as the words. At times, he was grand and over-the-top but, more often than not, he said it as if he were saying, "will the rain ever stop?" in a way that showed he didn't care if it did or did not. Pepper had never known anyone like Chatty. Even in the South, where characters are generously placed in big cities and little towns, Chatty was a character who couldn't be outdone.

Though, once when Pepper was an agent working out of his hometown of Memphis, he had been sent out to McNairy County, made famous by Sheriff Buford Pusser who was such a legend that his life became a blockbuster motion picture. Pusser was long dead by then, but the McNairy Sheriff had requested help in serving a warrant. That wasn't a normal request. It did happen from time to time but it was a bit unusual.

When Pepper got to the Sheriff's office in Selmer, he asked why the Marshals had been requested.

The Sheriff, Wayman Gooder, took off his glasses and wearily rubbed his eyes. "Because I'm black and my deputy's black. She says she don't like no black people. Her name is Ophelia Loggins."

"So, she's a racist," Pepper replied. The sheriff stood up from behind his grand metal desk—one that had been rumored to have belonged to Pusser, but no one was still alive who could vouch for that.

"Not exactly. She's a black racist but not against blacks." He rubbed his forehead. "It's complicated."

The Sheriff motioned to a metal seat that added no personality to the tiny basement office with light green painted cemented walls. Whenever Pepper glanced out the window, he saw boots and high heels walking by, between the bushes, down the sidewalk and could even see, through the oak trees, the clock on the old courthouse across the street.

"Sir, I'm confused."

Sheriff Gooder, one of the most respected law officers in the state of Tennessee, nodded. "Yep. I understand your confusion. Here's the twister—she's black." He took a pause as he watched the stunned look melt across the Marshal's face. "But she thinks she's white." He cleared his throat. "I want to say this as gently as possible. She's close to seventy-five now and ever since I was a little boy, people around here would say, 'she just ain't right.' Have you ever heard the mountain word 'tetched'?" Pepper's mind was still back at "she thinks she's white" so, stunned, he shook his head. "Oh, that's right," the Sheriff nodded, reminding himself. "You're a city boy. Memphis, right?"

Pepper nodded. "I had a second cousin who was a beauty queen and dated Elvis," he joked, a bit nervous, and Sheriff Gooder laughed heartily.

"That proves it. Any pretty woman from Memphis dated the King." Sheriff Gooder agreed, winding down from the big laugh to a small chuckle. "Up in the backwoods, people say that a person is 'tetched in the head' if they have an oddness or are simple-minded. By the way, I have found that these are the sweetest people in the world. That would not be

Ophelia. As the years go by, she gets worse. She thinks she's a snake charmer, a cancer healer and, if she likes you, she'll read your tea leaves and predict a grand future to come." He walked back to his chair behind the desk, sat down, leaned back and grinned. "Handsome, white, young man like you, she's sure to take a likin' to you. I don't foresee no trouble to come. Especially if you ask to have your tea leaves deciphered. Tell you what—I'll send my Deputy to trail behind you at a discrete distance, just to make good and certain that we return you to the US Marshal's office in Memphis."

Pepper was starting not to think much of this assignment. "What's the warrant for?"

"Well, we got us a good preacher over at the Antioch AME church. Me and my wife go there. We raised our children in that church. The good Reverend Randolph decided—against my best advice—that he'd go out and visit Ophelia and share the Lord with her. Now, don't get me wrong: we all agree that she could do with a good dose of the Gospel but you gotta get through the devil, first."

Pepper's mouth had long dried out, so he got up and walked over to the cooler and drank two cups of water. "I gather that Reverend Randolph went," he asked as he tossed the cup in the trashcan.

The Sheriff nodded as he picked up the receiver and toyed with untangling the cord on the old telephone colored in beige. "Didn't end too badly. It could have been lots worse. I guess the good Lord was with him." This was the perfect place for a dramatic pause and, being the fine storyteller that the Sheriff was, he did not disappoint. He watched Pepper's face for a few seconds then began again. "She showed up at the door with the old double-ought shotgun she carries everywhere. He was scared but introduced himself and said, 'I thought you might want to talk about the Lord." She narrowed her eyes and said, 'I ain't got nuthin' to say to Him and if I did, I'd do my own talkin'. Don't need a fancy-dressed preacher, that's for sure. Wait here a minute."

The Sheriff set the receiver, with the untangled cord, back in the cradle with the rotary dial. "When she come back, she was toting a brand new can of jonquil yellow paint. May be pretty on a flower but it ain't nuthin' but ugly when it's on a man of God. She threw the whole can on him. Some got in his eyes, so they had to work on him for a while over at the hospital but we agreed at prayer conference that night, that the Lord had, indeed, been with Preacher Randolph."

The explanation was paused while the Sheriff answered a call. Then his secretary, hobbling on a sprained foot, came in to ask for his lunch order. "Marshal, let me buy you lunch. It might be your last."

"No, thank you. I prefer to go out on an empty stomach. It'll make the autopsy easier."

The secretary left but Pepper, only two years out of training, was more than a bit nervous.

The Sheriff got up and walked around the desk where he sat down on the edge and put a reassuring hand on the Marshall's shoulder. "Buddy, it'll be okay. I'm not sending you into an ambush. My deputy will be there to back you up. But we can't have people disrespectin' a man of the cloth. Above all, we gotta respect the ones who preach the gospel. By the way, our church," he smiled sweetly, "done went and bought him a new suit, shirt and shoes. And socks. Two pairs."

Pepper took a deep breath, stood up and shook hands with Sheriff Gooder. "It's been a pleasure. I hope I can do what you need."

Gooder laughed heartily, holding his hand against his gut. "Oh, you can. You're the right color."

Pepper had his hand on the metal doorknob, about to open it, when Sheriff Gooder, chuckling, said, "Please, give Miss Loggins my best regards. Tell her I'd much appreciate her vote come next November." He grinned and winked.

"If you don't mind, sir, I don't believe I'll do that."

It was a case that Pepper would remember always, most especially because it went off without incident. No paint. No shotguns. About three years later, Sheriff Gooder called Pepper. "Marshal, I thought I'd share an unusual development with you. Something, somehow, has come over Ophelia Loggins. She woke up one morning and realized she is black and not white. She's even joined our church. Now, she's still not all there, if you know what I mean. She's got her quirks and smirks but all I can say is that heaven has brought forth a powerful change."

At a law officer conference, where Pepper was conducting a training session in recent years, he heard from one of the McNairy deputies that she died about ten years later but not before becoming one of the most devoted members of

Antioch AME Church. Curious, Pepper looked up her obituary in the paper and the last line said, "Her chocolate peanut butter cake is going to be missed mightily as will she."

Chapter Three

❦

Chatty, having been successfully derailed from the "beautiful" comment, or so Stella believed, but then again you never knew when it would pop into his head at a moment's notice, asked, "What brings you here, Pepper?"

"Chatham, I live here. Remember? In a condo on the north side," Pepper replied. He was wearing a blue striped, button-down shirt and a pair of navy slacks. Unless they ran into him at church, he was usually wearing a sports shirt with the monogramed logo of the US Marshals and a pair of khakis. "Most nights, I stop by for a beer or a burger or, sometimes on special occasions, I get both."

Chatty, knowing that Pepper was giving him a dose of his own kind of smart aleck, twisted his nose at him. He would have stuck out his tongue, but he learned better than that in the third grade when he stuck it out at Asher Bankwell and got a paddling from Mr. Cronic, the Principal, and that cured him forever more of doing any such. That dadgum Asher Bankwell. He had spent his life being a thorn in Chatty's side.

"Oh, but unlike the Apostle Paul, my thorn has been removed," Chatty gleefully declared the day that Asher was arraigned without bond enroute to the grand jury and, surely, an indictment. "Again, it is clear that my working faithfully on bingo with the elderly on Thursday nights at the church hall is really paying off. The good Lord watches after the faithful."

Stella, that evening at the King and Prince, was wearing a casual navy linen dress and espadrilles. She and Chatty had decided to grab dinner early before the hotel, which always had some conference going on, got too busy at the bar that was near the center of the lobby. It was always too loud there when folks, enjoying a few days on the company's expense account, came into the bar area, despite the spaciousness. She had failed, on purpose, to tell him that she had an appointment later than evening.

Chatty, always suspicious and, tonight, he was even nosier than his usual suspicion, looked from Pepper's striped shirt to Stella's dress. He gave a long, studied look to each. No one said anything for a moment until Chatty said to Stella, "Dahlin', the intuitive side of me which comes from my mother's family—after all, they were smart enough to build their grand houses here before Georgia was even a state—though from my sainted father comes most of the land in Colquitt County and surrounding area, tells me that something is going on here. Something that neither of you are telling your dear, sweet Chatty."

No one said a word. Pepper took a sip of water. Silence was the one thing that Chatham Balsam Colquitt IV could not tolerate. "Silence sours on my stomach," he would say now and again. It was one of his self-proclaimed "Chattisms."

"So. It's come to this," Chatty said in his haughtiest tone. "Let us not forget that most recently I am the one who saved both of your lives. *Both.* Without my quick finger on the trigger and my perfect aim, you two would be singing in the heavenly choir or, more likely, doing physical labor with some of the lesser angels. The ones who barely make it there."

"As usual, Chatham, you exaggerate," Stella replied.

He folded his arms across his chest, pushed his lips into a pout and looked away from his beloved Stella. In a few moments, he began to loosen up. Chatty, the clever one, had long ago figured out that acting hurt worked best with Stella. So, he unfolded his arms from across his broad chest attired in a peach-colored Ralph Lauren dress shirt and blue seersucker jacket, and turned the pout into a sad downturn at the corners of his mouth then placed his hand against his forehead.

"What have I done, Stellie, to deserve this? I love you more than anyone on earth. And maybe in heaven, too, because I'm not sure who I know who got there. My father for certain. So, I love you as much as Tripper Colquitt." He stopped to think for a moment: "My nanny used to say, 'T'aint it a wonder how the good Lord doeth work'? When I was little, Asher bullied me so my father stood up for me. Then, all these years later, I stood up for you with Asher." He sighed contentedly.

She reached over to touch his arm with her fingernails painted a peach color almost identical to his shirt.

"Chatty, I'm sorry. We weren't trying to keep anything from you. It just didn't come up."

"COME UP!" he exclaimed, throwing his arms in the air. "Things don't 'come up' between close friends. They're *told. Told, Stella, told!*"

A waiter came by and Pepper stopped him. "Jack Daniel's Black. And make it stiff. I think I'm gonna need it."

Chatty looked from Stella to Pepper to Stella again. Stella, in the meantime, looked down at the beautifully black and white inlaid marble floor. Then, she sighed with resignation and looked at Pepper. "I have to tell him."

Pepper nodded. Due to how close they were sitting to the bar and what good tippers they were, Pepper's drink arrived quickly, just in time to for him to take a long pull before Stella stepped into Chatty's whirlwind. "Only child syndrome" was what Stella called it since his sister had died before he was born. He was paranoid about being left out of anything. Even Stella, going to the grocery store without him, could send him off into an overplayed fit of sheer anguish.

"Remember, a couple of nights ago when Mrs. Puckett came out on the terrace to tell us about her nephew?"

"Nephew? What nephew?" Chatty asked, truly mystified. "I recall this not."

"It was at your birthday party. You came out on the terrace to find us?" Chatty was staring into the distance, squishing his eyes as if he were trying to make a staticky television come into focus. For a moment, Stella got caught up in the sideshow before shaking herself out of it and getting back to business.

"Okay, Chatty. Let's try it this way: we'll make it about you. Let me see if I can recall what you said under the starry night, something like: 'What are y'all doing out here? This is the celebration of the day that the good Lord, in all His wisdom, put me on this earth. Remember, this night—March 12th—is *all* about *me*.'"

Chatty nodded his head and shook a finger in agreement. "Which is true. It was all about me. I don't think, though, I said, 'in all His wisdom'" He paused for a second of thought. "But it *is* true. Now, back to now: What does that have to do with this deception I have hanging before me with such ugliness?"

Good manners or not, Stella reached into her purse and pulled out her lip gloss, gliding the light coral over her lips before speaking. "Mrs. Puckett—the same Mrs. Puckett who stuffs you—too much—with huge omelets was telling us there had been a murder on Sapelo Island and that her nephew had been arrested for the murder."

Chatty's hands flew to his mouths and his eyes bugged out. "Oh no! You don't say!"

Stella, knowing good, full and well, that Chatty had been standing there during the last part of the conversation was now annoyed. She was certain, also, that she'd mentioned going to the library to do research about Sapelo.

"Chatty, do you think about yourself *all* the time?" Stella shook her head in exasperation, her red curls bouncing vigorously.

Chatham Balsam Colquitt IV received the question without upset. Instead, he crossed one arm across his chest and placed a finger from the other hand under his chin. Pensively, he considered the question. She had meant it sarcastically, but he had taken it seriously. Pepper, amused, tried to hide a smile while Stella stared at Chatty, determined not to let him off the hook. Chatty looked down at the candle in the amber-colored container, centered on the white tablecloth, as he carefully considered it. Pepper was now close to choking with laughter, but Stella was not one bit amused. So, he turned his head and looked around the lobby, throwing up a hand at a fellow Marshal.

Finally, after a brief pause, Chatty spoke.

"Yes." He said it casually and with no shame attached. He punctuated the answer with a commonsensical nod.

Stella's mouth dropped open and Pepper burst into laughter. Stella glanced over at Pepper, with a frown. He quickly picked up the Jack Daniel's and took a slower sip.

"Don't encourage him," she reprimanded the Marshal. She then turned to Chatty who, unperturbed, was taking a sip of his dirty martini. Then, he took the toothpick that held two blue cheese stuffed olives and nibbled on one, quite enjoying himself.

"Chatty, you can't spend your entire life thinking only of yourself," she lectured.

Pulling an olive off the toothpick and not even bothering to look up at her, he replied, "Why not? Who else should I think of?"

"Let's begin with friends. People who are sick. Children in Africa without enough food. Churches, nonprofits, and the homeless. You have a lot of money that you can do good with."

He smiled and reached over to pat one of her hands that was gripping the table in near anger. "Dear, dear Stella what I mean is that I think of myself constantly, but I often have other people included in those thoughts. Like you and the Burnetts. Pepper, now and then." He looked over at Jackson Culpepper, winked and smiled mischievously. "In the spring, I'm always concerned about the Dooley Hydrangea that Coach Vince Dooley dug up right out of his yard and gave to me one hot August night. I was in Athens for dinner at their house. You know, Barbara and I are *good* friends. Not like Stella and me, but we're close." He looked over at Stella. "She loves you, of course, you know. So, if a spring freeze comes, I worry that the blooms will die for the year." He looked over at Stella then turned his head to the side and whispered, "Stella is too hard on me, sometimes."

Stella, hearing the whisper, asked, "What did you say?"

"Dahlin', I was clearing my throat. The pollen, you know. Barbara thinks the world of you, of course, as I'm sure you are aware. She was completely devastated when she heard how you had been treated by Asher and how I had to shoot the bad guys. Oh, I held Vince Dooley in such high regard just as highly as he held every Chatham or Colquitt who crossed his path. Do you think he can see down from heaven and know how my hydrangeas are doing and how kindly I treat them?"

With unfettered seriousness, he looked at Stella, a furrow wrinkling between his eyes. "It worries me something awful during those frigid nights." He studied on the brass railing leading down into the lobby. He had many things he could choose to say that would be powerful, but he wanted to choose his examples carefully. He needed to save some back, just in case he got in trouble again like this. And knowing Stella, she'd slip up on him again with the same accusation. Thank goodness, he had been a chess progeny who was taught by his grandfather Chatham, beginning at the age of five. "Always hold back an unexpected move," Grampy had said.

And so he did. But he did have one delicious move left to make for the current brow beating.

"I think about how I caught Mona Windsor cheating at bingo the other night, then I made certain to tell *everyone* at church and the country club because she's such a tell-tale herself. And, of all things, she did it—*she cheated—within the sacred walls of the church*." He paused and smiled sinisterly because he was about to deliver the big line. "Do unto others as they have done unto others."

Stella heaved heavily. "As usual, you have misquoted and turned it to your own service." She gave up. There was no use to go further because, regardless of what he said, Chatty was always there for her. If the Governor or Miss Alva was sick,

41

he was there at their disposal since they were childless. You could count on him for most anything except if it had to do with children and then *he did not have time.*

Chatty spoke in italics much of the time but when it came to children and asking him to help with Vacation Bible School or in an emergency, he spoke in both italics and caps such as, *"I DON'T DEAL WITH CHILDREN. THIS IS A CHOICE I MADE CONSCIOUSLY WHEN I CHOSE NOT TO MARRY. WOMEN ARE ALWAYS LOOKING TO GET YOUR MONEY AND TO PROCREATE SO THEY CAN KEEP YOUR MONEY!!"*

Once Mary Donovan was going to ask for a donation to the Biddle Society Rose Garden. She didn't know Chatham well so she asked Stella who lived across the park from her and with whom she sometimes played tennis at the club. THE club. The one that had wasted no time in scratching Stella's name from the roster. Later, they took off Asher's—a move that nearly killed Miss Caroline because Jasper's grandfather had been a founding member—and, in a show of graciousness, the club's President called Stella, apologized and asked if she would like to rejoin. Of course, she said "no" but played it off to her now living on St. Simons Island. She was enjoying life on the high road after having been dumped from the high life.

"I don't know Chatham well," said Mary following a volley with Stella during a tournament, "and since you do, I wanted to ask: Is there anything I should not discuss with him?

Stella always wore the cutest tennis dresses—it was fun for a mountain girl to play dress-up. In fact, she designed her own dresses, sometimes she sewed them and, other times, she had Mrs. Kilmont make them.

"You really need to stop wearing those homemade tennis clothes to the club," Chatty said one day while they were lunching at the club. He leaned forward with a conspiratorial tone. "People are talking."

She gave him a dead-eye level look. "I think they're lovely," she responded with a so-there-smile.

He shook his head. "That's the kind of thinking that got Cleopatra in trouble."

In such times with such ridiculous comments, Stella never bothered to answer. There is nothing to be said to some of the nonsense that Chatty makes up then carries forth as the truth.

Stella was just tossing the ball in the air as she heard the question. She hit it squarely to Mary's back left, grateful for the timing of the question. As it flew through the air toward the net, Stella yelled, "Children. Don't mention children!"

The answer startled Mary so much that she stood right where she was and didn't attempt to hit it. "Game, set, match," Stella called and, as she jogged toward the net for the traditional handshake, she thought, 'Chatty can be pretty useful at times.'

That highly-valued win came to mind and how she had gone on to win the club tournament because of Chatty's antics and off-centered thinking. So, there at the King and

Prince, as Pepper sipped on his drink, anticipating more entertainment, instead of pushing it further and suggesting, for instance, that he read the Bible instead of making it up, she let it go.

"Right, Chatty, you're right. Do unto others as they have done unto others. Right."

Chatty could always tell when he had worn her out so as soon as that skirmish was over, Chatty stirred up another one. He was not one for letting something go but, cleverly, he came at it from a different direction than before.

"Stella Faye, it's very unbecoming that you didn't think to put on pearls with that dress. I have trained you to be a proper Southern woman instead of some mountain hooligan. Have I not? What earrings do you have on? I can't tell with all that gorgeous amount of red hair covering your ears."

She looked at him blankly as the frantic truth scooted through her brain. She was in such a hurry when she dressed that she had not changed out a tiny pair of gold balls that she slept in. She liked having earrings on if she needed to dash out the door suddenly. In the morning or even in the middle of the night. That was a life lesson she had borrowed from her daddy and modified it a bit. Though she did adhere to the original lesson, too.

The lecture came back in the days of her teenage years when everyone she loved was still alive. Most importantly her daddy. Sims walked by the old junker of a Ford Pinto that had been bought with money earned by Stella over a year's worth of odd jobs then matched by her parents. She was sitting on the porch, a newspaper in her lap and a bowl by her side stringing beans, when Sims walked by her car and stopped at the gas tank. This was in the years when gas stations closed by nine and convenience stores were dark by ten.

"Stella Faye, how much gas have you got in that car?" He threw his head toward the awful-looking thing.

She shrugged. "Enough to get to school in the morning then to Junior's after class to get gas."

She could tell by the set of Sims's jaw that the answer did not set well with him. He went over, opened the door, sat down on the corner of the ripped beige leather seat, turned the ignition switch, and watched the gas gage. Aggravation flew across his face. He turned the ignition off and got out of the faded orange car that had a tiny crack in the top center of the windshield. Slowly counting down his temper, he walked over to the daughter that he adored just a little bit more than he adored her sister, Lynn.

"Little girl, let me tell you a thing or two. Listen to every word I tell you then keep it in your little pipe and smoke until it sticks with you real good." Stella turned pale. She never knew when she might get a lecture on something that Sims believed she should do but had never told her. Mountain people, especially those with "good, common, horse sense" as they liked to say, enjoyed holding center stage dramatically in times like these. Especially when they wanted something remembered. In his sternest, most theatrical voice, he began.

"From this moment forward, consider your car is on empty if it has half a tank of gas. When it gets to half a tank, stop and fill 'er up. Junior's got a crush on you so he will be glad to see you comin', anytime you stop by."

Sims looked at her hard. She questioned everything so he waited and, in less than five seconds, he was rewarded with "Why?"

"Because if we get a call in the middle of the night that someone is dyin' or someone needs to go to the hospital, every vehicle on this place is always gonna have half a tank of gas in it. Minimum. Understand? Even the tractors."

"Yes, sir."

And, from that late summer day forward, she did just that. Ironically, she would need to use that rule only twice: Once, when the call came to her University of Georgia dorm room toward midnight, that Sims had been injured badly by a hay baler. It took just a bit over an hour to drive from Athens to Gainesville, but she got there in time to sob "goodbye."

His rough, calloused-hand held hers as he whispered, "Stay close to the Lord. There'll be plenty of times you'll need Him. Take care of your Mama."

As usual, Sims Jackson was right—there were plenty of times when she needed the Lord but, also too many times when He wasn't as nearby as He should have been. It was she who had moved, not the Lord. The second time she used the Sims Jackson rule of gasoline economics was the night she escaped, with only seconds remaining, from Asher Bankwell and her former life in Buckhead.

She had come to apply that rule to her earrings. This murder and Campbell Puckett's predicament had occupied her mind all day. It had never occurred to her to change even when she stopped by the cottage to walk Spigot.

"Stella Bankwell." Chatty said it in a stern voice.

Biting her lip, she looked at him, wordlessly.

"Stella Faye, you're biting your lip. I know what that means. If you don't show me, I shall walk over and pull your hair back myself. Let's not make a scene here at the King and Prince. The one you made at the Buckhead Country Club will live in infamy. I think that's quite enough for one lifetime."

She glared at him and pulled back her hair on the right side. Chatty gasped, then clutched at his chest, crumbling the stiffly starched peach shirt in his hands as though he might have a heart attack. He closed his eyes and leaned his head backwards.

"My dear Jesus, please tell where I have gone adrift? How have I failed so miserably?" He cried woefully falling against his chair and fanning his face with a black napkin at if he was going to faint. It was quite a performance "And all those nights of church bingo, too."

"Oh, Chatty, quit it," she said, leveling her eyes at him. "I know what you're doing so let's stop the dramatics now and I will tell you where Pepper and I are going."

Chatty's woe immediately dissipated. He straightened up in his chair and smiled.

He rubbed his hands together joyfully. "So, let's get started. What are we waiting on?"

Chapter Four

CR

Chatty listened intently as Stella and Pepper explained what had happened and where they were going after dinner. He was so captivated that he did not once interrupt to comment or ask a question. He let his over-exaggerated expressions speak for themselves. He didn't even order desert.

"So, we're on our way to the Governor's and Miss Alva's to discuss his meeting with the District Attorney today and strategize our trip over to Sapelo Island tomorrow. The sheriff has agreed to let us into the crime scene as long as one of his officers and the Governor is with us," concluded Stella.

Chatty sat back in his chair, his arms crossed, and just shook his head. "That sounds like one of those murder mysteries on TV." From out of nowhere, he said, "I love Keith Morrison's voice and his storytelling. Isn't he the best?"

He could always easily take a story into another direction. Right now, Stella and Pepper were concerned about Campbell Puckett who, by all accounts of those who knew him, was a fine young man. He had recently graduated from a small college with a degree in engineering. He had received a small scholarship, a nice grant, and had worked one or two jobs at a time to pay the rest. His parents had given him as much as they could scrape together. His father, Jim, worked at Sea Island's The Lodge as a landscaper and his mother, Marianne, was a practical nurse. Campbell was the first in both of his families to graduate from college.

The Pucketts regularly attended Frederica Baptist Church where Jim served on an advisory board and Marianne headed up Vacation Bible School every summer. Campbell mentored teenage boys and then was available to volunteer for anything, any time he was needed. When Christ Church conducted its annual Tour of Homes, an enormous project as well as a huge fundraiser for the community, the ladies always knew that they could count on Campbell's help that weekend.

Happy was the day that Campbell landed a job with a highly respected contractor, Stewart Collingworth, who was based in Brunswick, across the causeway from St. Simons. Campbell dreamed of starting his own construction company someday. One of the men in their church—Collingworth's banker—recommended Campbell and he was immediately hired. He had been there for nine months and proven to be dependable, hard-working and kind to everyone around him.

"I'm going with you to the Burnetts'," Chatty said definitively. Stella didn't mind. She always liked to have her best friend around even when he was instructing or reprimanding her. She had to admit, she had become more worldly and more polished because of Chatham Balsam Colquitt IV even if he did drive her up the wall at times.

Jackson Culpepper, however, blanched at the declaration. He had not had an opportunity to be alone in private with Stella since the night they had almost kissed. While he shaved before going down to the restaurant, he thought of the opportunity he might have to kiss her when he took her home from the Governor's house. He tried to think of an excuse, but he knew that it was useless. It was hard to separate Stella from Chatty, who treated her like his prized possession. Chatty liked beautiful things and there was nothing, as far as Pepper was concerned, nor anyone more beautiful than Stella Bankwell. He had met her just across from where they were sitting, in the hallway of the King and Prince, when she had stopped to read the hotel's history. She looked like a porcelain doll so perfect in face and figure. But it was her sense of humor and sweetness that had really won his heart. Stella had, perhaps, the quickest wit he had ever encountered. She was even more fun to be with than to look at so that, right there, should tell you plenty. If his heart could be won, Stella was surely destined to be the winner.

After a traumatic shootout in which he had been involved, he was mandated to see a psychologist. It was there that he had been told that he was afraid of commitment. Though he denied it, when the evidence was laid out on the table—all the girlfriends who had passed through his life and the few who wanted desperately to marry him—the well-trained law officer had to admit to himself what he had always told his trainees at Glynco, the federal training facility in Brunswick: the evidence don't lie.

But he felt differently about Stella. His heart skipped a beat when he saw her. When he heard her voice on the phone, his day became brighter. Though she was newly-divorced and most would say she needed time to recover, this situation was different. The marriage had been badly troubled for a few years. Plus, Asher was having an affair as well as conducting an illegal business in which he had included his teenage son. He had no doubt: Stella was well over Asher Bankwell even though Pepper had seen him in court and had to admit that, despite his dastardly ways, he was handsome even in his prison orange.

Pepper, good naturedly sighed, and called for the check. Chatty always picked up the check. Always. It didn't matter if it was two people or twenty. He was gracious, almost to the point of being used by people. When the check arrived, Chatty reached for it but Pepper, pulling his billfold from his back pocket, waved him away.

"Chatty, this one's on me. For the entertainment value." Pepper winked with a grin and Chatty, who loved nothing more than to be bragged on, held his head up proudly as if he had just won an award.

Pepper helped Stella with her chair and said, "I'll grab the car and pull around to get y'all."

Chatty took Stella's arm as soon as Pepper was out of earshot and said, "He's a keeper. Asher Bankwell never picked up a check when I was around."

Stella, smoothing the wrinkles from the navy linen dress, laughed and said, "I figured that would win you over."

CR

Miss Alva answered the door of the Burnetts' expansive Sea Island home and, as usual, she was perfectly attired in a dark gray skirt and a pale green matching cardigan set. Chatty, at 6'2" and stout, hovered over 5'4" inch Stella, though her espadrilles added three inches, and Pepper, who was just a smidge over six feet tall. Chatty had weighed over ten pounds at birth—his mother claimed for the rest of her life that he had almost killed her which convinced her right then and there that he would be the last child delivered from her body—and, from that moment forth, he had been a well-fed child, splurging on whatever food brought him joy. He was always the largest child in class, something that the almost always unkind Asher Bankwell enjoyed pointing out. Once, in the first grade, Chatty had come home, sniffling over the taunts of Asher and his friends. His mother was on yet another jet-setting trip of hers, visiting Jackie Onassis on some Greek island where a select few had been invited.

His father, called Tripper since he was the third Colquitt, was home working when the sad little boy shuffled in and dropped his coat and books on a chair. Tripper was the compassionate, loving one of Chatty's parents. He had a parental instinct that his wife, Cecelia, did not have nor could she conjecture it up when Tripper had discussed the situation with her. Finally, he had accepted that she would never be motherly.

When he heard the sniffles as Chatty, head dropped, passed his office, Tripper had looked up from his work and called, "Hey, buddy, come here."

When he saw Chatty's red-rimmed eyes and noticed that his white shirt was half hanging out of his plaid shorts and vest—his school uniform—he was immediately concerned. He stood up from his desk, walked around to a small love seat, and sat down. "My dear pal, come over here and sit down. Let's have a talk."

Chatty dragged his feet over, wiping his eyes, and plopped down. He did not look at his father.

"Son, I've rarely seen you cry. What *is* wrong? Are you sick?"

Chatty shook his head full of dark brown hair and gave a sad heave. "Asher and his friends were making fun of me."

Immediately, Tripper felt anger rising up from his gut. Jasper Bankwell was a decent man who could always be counted on doing business ethically and treating people fairly. But Caroline Bankwell, the doyenne of Atlanta society, was raising her son in the most entitled way. Though the Bankwells were very rich, their fortune dating back to the mid-1800s, first made from railroad money, was almost a pittance compared to the Chathams and Colquitts. For the Chathams, Cecelia's family, and the Colquitts, their inherited fortunes first began in the 1700s, after the War of Independence, when there was significant opportunity with building that called on lumber, bricks and stone. All the Colquitts and Chathams—the Chathams of Savannah—who followed, adapted to the times, making money with whatever was needed back then. Railroads. Telegraph lines. Newspapers. And later, radio stations. Tripper's grandfather invested heavily in the stock market but that earlier patriarch, Chatty's great-grandfather, sold all his investments and took his profits at the end of 1928. For 10 months, his buddies at the exclusive men's club in downtown Atlanta, laughed at his caution as the market climbed astronomically but that Chatham—he was Chatham the first—said, "I'd rather make a one-hundred-dollar profit than take a ten-thousand dollar loss of hard-earned money."

When the stock market crash came in October of 1929, they laughed at him no more. One friend, Mason Cunningham, had jumped from the top of the Biltmore Hotel and left his wife and children poor and in desperate need. Though both families were cash and land rich, the Colquitts and Jasper Bankwell's Grandfather, thankfully, had sunk a good bit of money into Coca-Cola stock because Asa Candler, the entrepreneur who had bought the formula from pharmacist John Pemberton, was a good friend to both men. The Coca-Cola stockholders were solid in their investments—so much so that Asa Candler carried a huge briefcase of cash to the family bank in nearby Villa Rica when President Roosevelt closed the banks because of a run on them by scared people wanting cash during the Great Depression. Asa stood behind the counter and handed people their money. Because of Asa Candler it was the only bank in America not to close.

The Woodruff family had bought the formula and company from Candler years earlier and was making it into an international brand when the market crashed. It was almost like printing money, the way the company was going. So, everyone, particularly investment-savvy Atlantans like the Colquitts and Bankwells, survived nicely, using stock gains and dividends to make money in other places such as construction later in a booming Atlanta. Chatty and Asher attended the same exclusive private school and, to make matters worse for the tortured Chatty, they were also in Sunday School together at Peachtree Presbyterian Church. He couldn't escape from the boy, who was already displaying a tremendous array of handsomeness and arrogance.

Tripper reached and pulled his son over to him and set him up on his knee. "Tell me all about it."

Chatty rubbed his eyes and, holding back his sobs, explained that Asher and two of his friends had called him "fat" and laughed at him when Chatty tried to play see-saw with Thomas White. Chatty was so heavy that the rather tiny Thomas was left dangling in the air until a teacher could rush over and help gently lower Thomas to the ground.

Tripper's heart ached as he listened. After Chatty finished, he took a moment before speaking. "Chatham, you are not fat. You are husky."

"What does that mean?" Chatty asked, tilting his head. He loved his father very much and always hung onto his every word.

"That means you could grow up to be big and strong like Earl Campbell who is a running back for the Houston Oilers. Remember watching the game with me last Sunday, how he ran over all those other players and scored so many touchdowns?"

Chatty's tears were starting to dry and he nodded eagerly.

"Or you could be a cowboy like John Wayne. You like him, don't you?"

He nodded vigorously.

"Or you could be an Olympic weightlifter or a businessman like William Randolph Hearst. He was husky. But you know what else, Chatham?"

The little boy, with hero worship in his eyes for his father, shook his head.

"Not only can you be anything you want as long as you apply yourself, but you might grow tall and skinny."

"But I'm husky," he protested. Now, it was starting to sound like an honor the way that his father told it.

"Well, at your young age, it's often called 'baby fat'. Most of us have had it. It's nature way of keeping our bodies and bones healthy. But as you grow up, it sheds away. Here's the main lesson I want you to always remember: Be kind. Always. And share what you have with others."

Chatty's cherubic face lit up. "Today, at morning recess, I broke my orange popsicle in half and shared with Sarah Jean Cantrell. She must have forgot her money this morning and left it at home. Sometimes, she does that so I always share mine with her." He smiled impishly. "Daddy, she's so pretty. Almost as pretty as Mama."

At that moment, Tripper Colquitt knew his son would be just fine. Sarah Jean Cantrell was one of five scholarship students at the prestigious school. It was a secret from most people but he, as well as Jasper Bankwell, were both trustees and helped to select the recipients. Her father had been killed in the Vietnam War, toward the end, when her mother was four months expectant with Sarah Jean.

Tripper hugged his son tightly. "You're a very gallant man. I'm proud of you, son."

"What does gallant mean?"

"Remember when we watched the movie where John Wayne picked up the beautiful woman and carried her over the large mud hole so her dress wouldn't be soiled? That was gallant."

Chatham Balsam Colquitt IV smiled broadly and said, "I'm going to treat Sarah Jean gallant again!" Returned to happy by his father's wisdom, he hugged his neck, jumped down and said, "I have to go or I'll miss the Mike Douglas Show. I have to get my bowl of ice cream first."

That night after homework, dinner and an hour's worth of television, Tripper Colquitt said prayers with his little boy and tucked him in. Then, he went to his study, closed the door and called Jasper Bankwell. He explained what happened and Jasper, painfully aware of his son's personality, was almost as upset as his friend.

"Tripper, I will take care of this immediately. I extend my most sincere apologies for how our son has represented himself and our family. Asher will get a serious punishment for this and his mother and I will have a come-to-Jesus meeting. When I'm not looking, she lets him get away with murder." Of course, he meant that figuratively but 30 years down the road, when a man named Bennett Sutton was killed, it became literal. Stella, knowing what a decent, well respected man Mr. Bankwell had been, often thought how glad she was that he had not lived to see the criminal his son became.

As for that first-grade situation, that was most of the last trouble Chatty ever had with Asher except for the times when he stole a girl away from Chatty or short-sheeted his bed at camp. Asher seemed to have learned his lesson well after the phone call between the fathers. And, too, from that moment forward, Chatham Balsam Colquitt IV was proud of his huskiness. "I'm just like John Wayne," he would often say.

C&R

Governor McCager Burnett—Governor being a courtesy title because, though he had been a Congressman for twelve years and a Governor for eight, it is common etiquette, to use the highest-ranking title—was sitting at the dining room table with papers spread before him. His glasses were resting halfway down his nose. He pulled the wire from over one ear and then the other when he saw the group come in then stood up. Cager was from the old school. He was often dressed, at home, in casual pants, a nice shirt such as the yellow striped button-down, paired with a yellow cardigan, buttoned at the waist by two buttons.

"Hello, Marshal," he said as he reached across the table while Stella walked around the table and hugged him as she had done, too, with Miss Alva. Chatty, comically, held up his opened hand and did a circular wave and a wink.

"Chatham, I wasn't expecting you," the Governor said lightly then chuckled. "But I have come to know that wherever Stella goes, you go, if it is in the least possible way for you to trail behind."

Chatty shrugged and smiled good naturedly and, rewriting the words to an old commercial jingle, sang, "I am stuck on Stella 'cause Stella's stuck on me!"

They all laughed and Miss Alva, as usual, said, "Let me make coffee. Mrs. Puckett baked her beloved spiced, raisin cookies this afternoon, knowing y'all were coming. She's so grateful for your help with Campbell." She disappeared through the swinging door and into the kitchen.

"Have a seat," the Governor said, motioning to the chairs. "Let's get down to the business of murder."

Pepper reached over and pulled out the chair for Stella, then each man sat on either side of her. Cager held a smile to himself. He had been thinking how happy that Chatty had been since Asher and Stella split and he had Stella to himself. Should Stella ever find another beau, Chatty was certain to be devastated. But now was not the time for frivolous thoughts of crushes or love. This was serious.

Cager began, explaining that the day after the murder, they had allowed the Governor to speak with Campbell but, just today, two days later, he had been able to get a bond hearing.

"I was a bit worried that there might not be a bond at all, despite Campbell's outstanding record as a person coupled with the fact that he's never even had a speeding ticket." McCager chuckled. "Of course, on the islands, it's a little hard to speed but he could speed up on Highway 17 between Darien and Brunswick."

"It seems to me that bail would be easy," Stella commented.

Pepper spoke up. He had seen too much of this—the imbalance of the legal system—in his almost twenty years of being a US Marshal. Though he was working in training at Glynco—an assignment he had asked to be increased from six months to a year after he realized his feelings for Stella— he had been in the field for many years. He scratched at the corner of his forehead near his blonde hair.

"If I were to guess, it has to do with the victim being a prominent CEO in a Wall Street traded company."

Cager nodded. "Exactly correct, Culpepper. Poor boy. If Campbell had to depend on an inexperienced attorney, a public defender or someone with no political clout, he might be in jail for two years IF he were indicted and were waiting for trial in a backed-up calendar. As our luck would have it, I was the Governor who appointed Jensen Duncannon to his judgeship when the previous Judge, unfortunately, suffered a stroke. When the next election came up, Jensen had to run for his position and won easily. He's now in his third term."

"So, you got him bond that got him released, at least, until grand jury and a possible indictment?" Pepper asked.

The Judge nodded. It had to be a fair bail so that no untoward accusations could be brought between the Governor and the judge.

"How much was the bond?" Chatty popped up to ask. Money always interested him.

"It was $250,000. I expected $500,000 to $750,000 but in less affluent counties like McIntosh, where the supposed murder occurred, it is not uncommon to have a lower bond. Georgia law says the alleged criminal has the right to have an affordable bond to get out of jail. Of course, it usually takes two or three bond hearings to get it down that low."

"But, Governor, it might as well be $2 million!" Stella exclaimed.

Alva Burnett pushed open the kitchen door, bringing out a silver tray with a silver coffee pot, creamer, sugar, beautiful china cups and saucers nesting together, and a silver dish with a paper doily and stack of cookies. She had come in, just in time to hear McCager—she always called him that—as he was discussing the bond. She set the tray down and began to pass the cups and saucers.

"I paid the bond," she said without pride, setting a cup and saucer in front of Stella. She said it as calmly as if she were talking about buying a carton of milk. She made no big deal of it. She simply finished putting the cups and saucers out then went to pick up the silver platter of cookies which looked so fetching in the midst of the dining room with blue silk wallpaper and matching silvery-blue window treatments of full-length drapes that pooled down on the Cyprus wood floor, an expensive wood not easily found anymore and certainly the sturdiest and prettiest of wood.

Chatty, much beloved by the Burnetts and vice versa, was always respectful and didn't carry on as he did with everyone else. He kept his mouth shut though it took all his might. Pepper certainly couldn't ask so the task fell to Stella. Both men looked at her.

"Miss Alva, you paid the bond?" She looked at the Governor. "Why did Miss Alva pay it but not you?"

She knew the Burnetts had great wealth and, as with all things with them, everything was shared.

"I plan to oversee the representation of Campbell, though that's not my area of expertise. I need a high-powered, smart defense attorney. A high percentage of murder suspects use public defenders. This is a specialty, far out of my reach. If Campbell is indicted and this goes to court, it'll drag on for weeks. It will be a high-profile case and the attorneys will enjoy the free publicity from the media. It could be as much as one million dollars." He paused for that surprise to sink in. Stella gave a faint gasp, but the men were unreadable. He waved away her concern. "But I started out as a trial lawyer before I decided that it would be much more fun to watch families arguing over estates. Oh, the stories I could tell about that." He laughed. "We have someone in the office, about seven years out of law school. We can let him work on this, pro bono, because we do a certain amount annually. If I need some guidance, I can make a phone call or two to expert attorneys or pull out the old law books. But when you're dealing with this kind of wealth, a high-profile victim, and the suspect is a good-looking white boy from South Georgia, the courtroom won't be able to seat all the media."

He rubbed his forehead. "Darn migraine. But back to bond. Having appointed the judge, I thought we might be pushing it too far for me to put up the money. A conflict of interest. If this goes to trial, and I fully expect there will be an indictment, the way things are looking, I feel certain that Jensen will recuse himself. That's always a worry because you never know who'll you get. It's especially worrisome when you've been in politics. It might be someone that I made awfully mad one time. Or more. I was trying to figure out the solution when my sweetheart, as she often does, had an answer."

The day before, Miss Alva had overheard a conversation between McCager and one of his law partners. The discussion was the bond which had been set that morning and how they were going to get the boy out of jail. When he hung up, Miss Alva softly entered the room, her black, rubber-soled loafers making not a sound. McCager was sitting in one of the club chairs in the living room. He took off his glasses and rubbed his eyes. She sat down on the sofa close to him. Mrs. Puckett had been with them for 30 years, since she was a young woman. She was more than a housekeeper or employee. She was a member of the family. Every year for Christmas, the Burnetts gave her a large bonus and extravagant presents for her and her husband, Delbert. They had known Campbell since he was born. Over the past few years, he often stopped by to change a lightbulb since the doctor had insisted that McCager, at his age, was not to be on a ladder. If the pool guy was out of town, Campbell took over. He was always happy to help and, often, Miss Alva had said to Mrs. Puckett, "That sweet Campbell has such a servant's heart. And the prettiest dark blue eyes. I've never seen eyes that color."

Mrs. Puckett always nodded in agreement. Once, she had explained that he was named after his mother's father, Campbell Taylor, who had served as a missionary in the Appalachian backwoods, where he'd seen untold poverty that changed his heart forever. He came back to South Georgia to pastor a small Baptist church in nearby Jessup.

When Alva sat down by McCager, she put her left hand on his hand. Despite the wealth they had amassed, she still wore her original, slim gold engagement ring with a tiny stone in it paired with an equally slim wedding band. McCager had always offered a bigger ring and she steadfastly refused. Once, for their anniversary, he had stealthily bought a four-carat diamond ring. He was tempted by the six-carat but knew she would refuse that. He was pushing his luck as it was.

He smiled proudly as she opened the fancy, wrapped package. Then his smile faded when her face fell. Tears filled her eyes.

"McCager, what is this?"

"An engagement ring to replace that little one I paid $40 for." He was rather sheepish.

"Forty dollars that you worked for almost a year to earn and save. You sold sheet metal, junk, mowed yards, anything you could do as you were finishing law school. This ring means the world to me for that." She took her other hand, held her left in it, and pressed both hands to her heart. Nothing could ever mean more."

McCager was too embarrassed to take the ring back to Sol Brownstein with whom he had done business for years and had even represented his daughter in an unseemly divorce case. He convinced Miss Alva to keep the ring even if she never wore it. She agreed. But to please him, on occasion when they had dinner with big, wealthy clients, she did wear it. Otherwise, it was in a safe in their home in Atlanta on West Paces Road. Ironically, it was two doors down from the Governor's mansion which proved surprisingly handy when McCager became Governor. And, even more ironically, Chatham was across the street and three doors down. On Sea Island, their houses were next to each other, but Chatham's was on the backside. He and Miss Alva adored each other so much that they had put a gate in the hedges between their houses so they could slip back and forth easily. The Burnetts were childless and Chatty was an orphan so it was a wonderful family that they made. One, that now included Stella.

Chatty spoke. "You put up $250,000 for Campbell Puckett's bond?" He was stunned. Miss Alva was a woman of good taste but always frugal. McCager liked to say that she acted just like a woman who would have been from Tur-niptown, the place of his upbringing. She had grown up in the slightly larger town of Cleveland, two counties over from McCager, and one county down from Stella. So they were all mountain people though you'd never know it by their looks now and how the society people fell all over themselves to get to them at parties. Momentarily, Stella's stock had gone down but when she discovered the money that Asher and An-nabelle had stolen as well as the offshore island where it was stored, she had become a celebrity and was appreciated mightily.

"Wealthy people," Cager had said at the time. "Every-thing comes down to dollars for them. Especially the ones born into it."

Miss Alva was slow to speak. She glanced over to McCager—she was the only person in the world who always called him McCager. Her husband looked at her and silently, slightly nodded.

"When my father died, he owned a few acres outside of Brunswick. When my brother died, a few years ago, with an aneurysm, he left his half of the land to me. It was kind of him because he had two children, but he knew that I had willed my share to him. As it happens, we had the land ap-praised several months ago. It's worth $285,000. In the state of Georgia, you can use land for a bond. No one in the Puck-ett family could afford the bond. So, when I heard McCager on the phone, I knew what I needed to do. Fortunately, I had the deed here, since we used a local appraiser, so I was able to put the deed up."

Chatty, logical and tactful as always, said, "What if he jumps bail and you lose your land?" He steadied his elbow on the table, put his hand in his chin and watched her carefully.

Stella spoke. "Chatty."

"What?"

"Again, everything is not about money. It's often about helping those who need help." Stella gave him the stern look she had learned from her Mama, the one that meant "stop your antics right now."

Miss Alva, as kind and mindful as always, said, "Chatty, sometimes, in our hearts, we know what we should do or what the Lord expects of us. I knew this was something I needed to do."

She did not explain but she had asked McCager about this in a conversation between themselves earlier that morning and he agreed. The land was important to her since her father had bought it. Part of her father lived on in that land. They were sitting in the living room, having a cup of coffee when she asked.

"You know there's a chance—albeit small, I believe—that you could lose that land if Campbell gets scared and skips the country?"

With a lump in her throat, she nodded. "McCager, may I ask you something?"

"Of course."

"If, for any reason that he jumps bond which I don't believe he would do," she took a breath, her heart beating fast, "Would you be angry if I sold that big diamond ring you gave me several years ago and used it to keep the land?"

McCager took a couple of moments to answer. He looked at her for a long time, studying the sincerity in her face and the longer he looked, the more the tears welled up in her eyes. Finally, he got up from his seat and went over to sit down beside her. He put his arm around her and pulled her close to him.

"Miss Alva, you've stood beside me for many years. You've had to sit through hundreds of Rotary meetings, dozens of Kiwanis gatherings, even more political this and that. I've always appreciated you but until this moment in time, I have never been prouder of you. He put his other arm around her and hugged her tightly as she sniffed. "I know how much that land means to you and this makes you mean even more to me—if that is possible."

"Then, may I do it?"

McCager looked up at the tall windows across the room with the sun streaming in. His heart had already surrendered but his legal mind took over. Was it a conflict of interest if Miss Alva gave the money? Something suddenly occurred to him. He snapped his fingers.

"My dear darling, there may be an answer to this."

He walked over to the white French Provencial desk, surrounded by built-in bookshelves which held only a portion of the books they possessed. He opened a drawer and pulled out an address book. The Burnetts still clung to the use of phone numbers and addresses written down, although they also had phone numbers stored in their phones. He dialed the cell number to Tom Everett, the trust lawyer in McCager's office, who handled his and Miss Alva's wills and trust.

"Tom, Cager here. Question: That piece of land that Miss Alva owns down in Brunswick?" He listened. "Yes, the one she had with her brother. Is that set up in the LLC where we put three or four pieces of property? Oh, it's in one by itself? Why? I didn't realize that."

Everett explained, "I set up a new trust because that piece was so special to her and you wanted to keep it as something that was strictly her own. I mentioned it to you, but you said, 'Do what's best. No need to run it by me. Just you and Miss Alva handle.'"

"Yes, I do recall that now. Good job, Tom. You have no idea how well you've done."

He hung up the phone and explained everything to Miss Alva but now the three who were sitting at their dining room table were eager to know.

"Miss Alva," said her husband. "You tell them."

She smiled a bit shyly. She wasn't used to being the center of attention. "When McCager and I first married, I worked at a bank to pay our rent and utilities while he was in law school. There were many years when we struggled to get by. As a young lawyer, he made very little. Then, just as he started to make enough money where we could save, he ran for Congress. That limited significantly how much he could

70

work at the firm. We've always tried to avoid the look of anything politically inappropriate. You know McCager is a man of great honor." She stopped and smiled at her husband. She straightened her pale green cardigan then continued.

"For six months out of the year, I worked for my cousin in his apple orchard and barns in Ellijay. I picked apples every year, then I worked in the family store, selling, or in the kitchen making fried apple pies."

Chatty just couldn't hold it in any longer. He had gone silent for much too long as it was. "Miss Alva, as we all know, I possess a strong intellect but, here, I find myself a bit flummoxed. How are we comparing apples to apples?" At this small joke, Chatty laughed gaily, holding his round stomach with both hands as he laughed.

"Chatham, please, extend Miss Alva the courtesy of finishing her story," the Governor said a bit gruffly. Chatty's face reddened. McCager Burnett was the only person on earth who could ever reel in Chatty and bring him to a complete stop.

"Excuse me," he said, quietly.

"Dear Chatty, it's quite fine. I can take a long time to get to the point." This wasn't true but Miss Alva was always quick to save a situation and make others feel better. "Here's the short: When my brother and I inherited that land, it was all he had when he died. We had sold his little house and small farm to pay for the nursing home and, even after that, McCager and I often picked up expenses since my brother, who had worked in a sawmill all his life, didn't have the financial means that we had."

She took a sip of coffee for no other reason than to hold herself together. Gingerly, she set the cup down on the saucer. "McCager said, 'This is all you've ever had that was all yours. A person needs a piece of dirt that belongs solely to them. I want you to have only your name on it. I haven't earned the right.' We turned it over to Tom Everett in McCager's firm. This Internet world has changed life for everyone. People can find out where you live and what you own. With that in mind, Tom set up an LLC that belongs to me but can't be searched through by people curious to know what we own. That made it absolutely perfect to use the land for bail for Campbell, without anyone knowing to whom it belongs."

"And, if they ever do find out," McCager concluded. "It will have taken a lot of digging." He paused. "I took a strong, ethical accounting of this before I agreed for Miss Alva to do it. But that land belongs to her. I don't have one penny in it. In fact, in her will, she plans to leave the land to her nephews. It will never belong to me."

No one noticed it. If they had, perhaps they would have thought that Chatty was sick. While the four others talked of the murder on Sapelo, the one with which Campbell Puckett had been charged, Chatty was silent. Normally, Chatty would have been fully involved with all the chatter which he viewed as gossip.

Instead, he sat quietly at the end of the table and was thinking seriously to himself.

Chapter Five

CR

Stella was trying to wash the grogginess out of her eyes during a second cup of coffee when Spigot scratched on the back screen door, indicating she was ready for her morning time outside followed by her morning breakfast. She was also eager for some cuddling which she got from Stella while having her morning coffee.

As Stella was mixing together Spigot's dry and wet food, the phone rang on the glossy blue, little table—the old-fashioned kind with a chair attached. Stella picked up the phone to hear Pepper's cheerful voice. He had been up since five and taken a long run on the beach so he was in prime condition.

"Hello, beautiful!" he called out.

"Ha-ha. I know that's an ode to Chatty and his take on 'beautiful'," she replied.

"It comes from the heart," he said without a second's pause. He was thankful to Chatty because he had made it possible to flirt easier with this gorgeous rose of a woman.

Pepper, after a chuckle, continued. "I wanted to make sure you're up and ready for your day's adventure on Sapelo."

Stella hated to admit it to herself, but she had become a bit of a tony Buckhead wife. Even for the last month, as she had helped Marlo out at the real estate office, she didn't have to be there until 9 a.m. When she set the pewter, jingling clock last night, she had tried to remember the last time she got up at 6:30 a.m. And she couldn't recall it at all. Asher, before his recent incarceration, had co-owned a jet company so they used it at whatever time they chose for take-off. And it was definitely not before 10 a.m.

"I'm getting there," she admitted. "I'm on my second cup of coffee and Spigot has been out. Marlo is going to come by and take care of her until we get back, tomorrow." She chuckled. "This is where it comes in mighty handy to have a best friend married to a veterinarian. She said that Spigot would be a welcomed guest at their abode as long as desired."

"Better pack an extra pair of slacks and a top." He had almost said "underwear" before realizing that they didn't know each other that well. "I've made enough trips like this to know you can never be sure when you might return."

"Great," she mumbled. Here, again, she hated to admit that she had grown used to a comfy life. She was a mountain girl. She had herded cows, baled hay in the searing heat, helped her Mama grow a vegetable garden, raised horses on a bottle when they couldn't get milk from their mamas, climbed atop the house to position the antennae, and had been eaten from her toes to her knees by fire ants. She had also experienced the joys of mountain life—heaps of mountain laurel, crickets singing on a summer's night, while they sat on the front porch in a swing or rocking chairs and just listened while watching the stars. At Turner's Corner, they didn't have to worry with "keeping up". No one worried about what someone else wore (it was all mostly homemade anyway) or who had the newest, finest car because, for the most part, everyone drove old pick-up trucks. But too much of the good life had rubbed off on her.

Sims, her father, would be so ashamed of his daughter if he knew she had grown accustomed to a luxury life.

Now, she and Jackson Culpepper were headed to Sapelo Island, one of Georgia's barrier islands and a place filled with history, mystery, and wildlife. Thomas Spalding, a cotton grower, was among the first to develop Sea Island cotton, known for an extra-long staple yarn and for being super fine in texture. Spalding, a pioneer in building with tabby, made with cement and crushed oyster shells, raised buildings on Sapelo with the tabby, some still standing over 200 years later. He died in 1851, having outlived five sons and a wife, before the Civil War would cause an upheaval of Sapelo, the South, and the entire nation.

The previous day, as the Governor and Miss Alva were working to arrange bond for Campbell, Stella had stopped by the library, just a stone's throw from Sloan's Realty on Mallory where Marlo worked with her in-laws as a realtor. Stella was helping in the office until their receptionist returned from maternity leave. She read as much as she could find on Sapelo. Stella, having discovered she quite enjoyed not having a smartphone during the days that she was hiding from Asher, now had a little flip phone. So, thank goodness that libraries still existed.

When she ran across the name, Howard Coffin, it rang a bell but she couldn't place it. He had bought Sapelo Island in 1911, after discovering it when he came down to Savannah for motor car racing. Her head bounced up. She reached into the pocket of the navy pants, paired with a red gingham peasant top, and pulled out a red leather notepad with a small pencil and jotted down his name. Upon returning to the office, she planned to dive onto the computer the desk she was using and learn more.

After graduating from the University of Georgia, Stella had gone to work for a sports marketing firm. Accidentally, she had found her sweet spot to be in motorsports so she worked as an account executive for companies involved in Formula One, Indy car, stock car, and drag racing. Somewhere, she had heard the name Coffin. She grabbed the notepad and hurried back to her office which, thankfully, she found empty except for Marlo who was on a conference call.

Hastily, she typed in "Howard Coffin" and found a connection between him, Sapelo, Sea Island and, most amazingly, the Hudson Car company. Most women of a young age had never heard of Hudson but Stella had spent a good portion of five years involved in the stock car racing circuit where guys like Richard Petty, Darrell Waltrip, and Richard Childress told fascinating stories of the sport's early glory days—such as when they raced on the beach in Daytona, then finally on asphalt in Darlington, Atlanta, Daytona, North Wilkesboro, and on and on.

The Hudson Hornet! Stella smacked her head. It was one of the most famous stock cars ever raced. Over and over, she had heard the guys mention the car which earned the nickname of the Fabulous Hudson Hornet because of its success with drivers like Herb Thomas. And Tim Flock? Didn't he drive a Hudson Hornet with his sidekick, a monkey named Jocko Flocko? She laughed to herself. All the guys had said that Jocko Flocko, perhaps loved the speed as much as any driver. It worked well until Jocko pulled some little stunt that allowed Tim to have an advantage, but only momentarily. The sanctioning body demanded that Flock come into the pits and give Jocko to them, a move that cost Tim the win. That's one story. Another claimed that Jocko had almost caused Flock to wreck by blocking his vision through the left side of the window shield. Both stories agree that Flock had to pit, remove Jocko from the car, and settle for third place. It was the end of Jocko Flocko's racing days.

While Pepper was talking about the weather, a memory of sweetness played across Stella's mind and she indulged it, enjoy the nostalgic look back. On a lovely fall day, just as the leaves were turning to stunning jewel colors of yellow, red, and orange, and race fans, attired in tee shirts of their favorite driver and toting huge coolers, were piling into Charlotte Motor Speedway, Stella had met the famous Tim Flock. She was on the outside of the track, checking on her client's tent and catering for the following day. A handsome, older man was setting up a camping tent nearby.

"Young lady, if you need any help over there, just let me know." He had walked a few feet closer and called to her. "You're awful tiny to be moving those tables around like that. Especially on grass."

She laughed. "I always know I'm in the South when I meet such gallant gentlemen. Thank you."

He was dressed in matching khaki pants and a shirt, wearing rubber-soled boots. He looked like the gas station manager of her youth. Suddenly, afternoon practice had begun, and they both stopped to listen while the cars zipped by, changing gears as they came out of the fourth turn.

He looked up toward the high embanked track and smiled sadly. "Ain't nothin' like the sound of that."

It was the wistful look of yesterday that played across the man's face and a sadness that filled his eyes. He was at least forty years older than Stella but, without question, he was one of the most handsome men she had ever met. Jet black hair, azure blue eyes, an angular face that was deeply tanned, and teeth brighter than pearls. He looked like a movie star from the 1940s. The sorrow in his eyes touched her heart. Stella walked over and held out her hand, "I'm Stella. I work for a sports marketing firm that does things like this," she said gesturing, throwing a finger over her back to the tables.

He took her hand and offered a brilliant smile. "A pretty girl like you should have boys fightin' ever which-a-way. Tell you what: If I were about 25 years younger, I'd be fightin' for your attention. Yes, siree. No question 'bout that."

Stella wasn't comfortable with compliments about her looks. Her Mama taught her that, always saying," Pretty is as pretty does. It's what's on the inside that counts."

She blushed and lowered her eyes. "Thank you." She searched to switch the subject. "Do you camp outside for every race here?"

He shrugged. "Not much." She thought she saw a lump form in his throat. He spoke and she heard it in his voice. "When memories are too good, you don't want to go around spoilin' 'em too much." He winked. "Oh, forgive my manners. I'm Tim." He paused a second. Later she would remember that pause and realize what it meant: if she knew who he was, it would lift his spirits. But if she didn't, it'd break his heart a little more than the sound of tires on the asphalt. Finally, he threw in the towel. "Tim Flock."

He happened to be standing in front of a young woman with a "sticky memory" as she called it. If Stella had read, heard, or seen anything, she could recall it, usually quickly. But sometimes, she had to relax and let it flow to the forward of her mind.

True astonishment covered her face. "You're the famous Tim Flock? Jocko Flocko, right?"

She had just made an old warrior's day. "Yep, that'd be me." He grinned. "Best partner I ever had, that Jocko. Better even than the fast Hudson Hornet." Stella looked at him for several seconds and realized that all she had heard was right—

Tim Flock, who was now up in his sixties—was an incredibly gorgeous man. They talked for a half hour until Stella had to leave for a meeting. As she walked away, her heart was a bit downcast because some of his sadness had rubbed off on her.

Stella now racked her brain, trying to recall for certain but she thought they had even raced a convertible version of the Hudson. She snapped her fingers again. Of course! The hit animated movie, *Cars*, had featured the voiceover of actor Paul Newman as Doc Hudson, a tip of the hat to the famous car.

Coffin, a motor car engineer, along with department store mogul, Joseph Hudson, and six other individuals founded the company in 1909. Coffin and another engineer, Roy Chapin, had left the Olds Motor Works to become the key designers of the Hudson, the first lower-priced motor car on the market. That development made all the investors into millionaires, including Coffin and Chapin, many times over. By 1951, it was the star of the stock car arena. Stella sat back in her chair, folded her arms and smiled, warmed by the memories of her racing days. One of her buddies had been Chocolate Myers, the fueler for Dale Earnhardt's car. Chocolate was tall and very strong which made carrying the fuel can over the wall a piece of cake. He and Richard Childress, who was always so kind to her when she worked the circuit, had been friends—probably as far back as childhood. A thought hit her, and she typed quickly again. Yep. She was right. Chocolate's father. Bobby, a well-known racer, had once driven a Hudson. He had been killed in a race accident in Darlington when Chocolate was a little boy.

"Small world," she said aloud.

"What?" asked Marlo as she passed by, headed toward the coffee pot.

"I was looking up some history of Sapelo because Pepper and I are going over there tomorrow, to look into this murder that Mrs. Puckett's nephew is accused of committing. Have you ever heard of the name Howard Coffin?"

Marlo, dressed simply in a light blue sheath trimmed in red rickrack, poured cream in her coffee and nodded her head. "Quite certainly. And anyone else who is a member of Sea Island has heard of him."

Stella swirled around in her chair and looked at her agog. "Sea Island?"

"Howard Coffin built the causeway to the little island sometime in the mid-1920s, I think. Then, he built the original Cloister. It was torn down several years ago and replaced with the magnificent one that's there now. You know where that enormous fireplace is in the lobby?" Stella nodded. "On one side is the library. And beside that door is a huge portrait of Howard Coffin."

"Of course," Stella said. It was all coming together for her. In the same way that she had met Pepper while reading the historical documents at the King and Prince, she had, whenever possible, studied the old black and white photos of the Cloister in its early days. That was where she had first seen the name Howard Coffin.

"Did he also own Sapelo Island?"

Marlo threw her head toward the door. "Here comes Tatum's Daddy. Ask him. He grew up here and has 70 more years of knowledge than I have."

Alton Sloan was whistling as he opened the door and walked in happily, swinging his arms as he went. He had made a fortune in island real estate so there was plenty of reason for him to always be happy.

"Good day, lovely ladies." He bowed and made a large sweeping motion with his right arm. Alton caused Stella to smile, just by looking at him. His pale blue eyes twinkled, casting a light all over his face and he was terrifically kind, always ready with a compliment.

Marlo loved her in-laws. Tatum's mother, Evelyn, was always clucking around everyone, taking pure pleasure in making someone's day better with a homemade coconut pie or lasagna. And, too, you could always count on her to be on quick dial as a babysitter for anyone on the island. Tatum, Marlo's husband, had a sister, Katherine Sloan Butterfield, who was a lawyer in Jacksonville. Together, they often laughed about their college days and how a trip home from school was usually guaranteed to find that a new foster baby was being sheltered in one of their bedrooms. Finally, Alton had said, "Evelyn, what you're doing is a fine contribution to society and I know it means a lot to you. But soon, you'll be too old to take in babies and chase toddlers around. Let's put you to work, selling real estate."

Reluctantly, she agreed—and it turned out to be a wise decision. In the first year, she ranked 25th on the list of top realtors in the entire state. Then, of course, they brought in Marlo when she and Tate married so she managed their rental programs and sold real estate, too. In exchange for her adorable cottage, Stella was helping out here, at the office, but now that there had been a murder of a pharmaceutical executive on Sapelo, understandingly, they agreed for her to take the time she needed to help Pepper with the investigation.

"Alton, what was the connection between Howard Coffin and Sapelo?" asked Marlo as she poured him a cup of coffee, as well, while he sifted through his messages.

"Howard? Oh, he owned Sapelo before selling it to R.J. Reynolds, Jr." Alton was too young to have known the Detroit wizard but his father, Al, had often hunted with him on land about 30 minutes away. Owned by Sea Island, it was a wonderland of wildlife and offered gentlemanly hunting on 1800 acres of marshland, tidal creeks, and forests.

Stella's mouth dropped. Another connection to her racing days. When she first showed up on the stock car circuit, it was sponsored by R.J. Reynolds' Winston brand, in the long-ago time when tobacco companies were allowed to advertise. The influx of cash that R.J.R brought into a sport was a game changer for all the racers because the purses went up as well as the championship money. Good racers, no longer barely survived, they thrived in great health, and went from driving vans to the races to flying in private planes.

"Howard Coffin owned Sapelo then sold it to R.J.R?" Stella asked in a stunned voice.

"What's remarkable about that?"

"Mr. Coffin was one of the chief engineers behind the Hudson Hornet race car which is still talked about in racing circles. Decades later, it was named the Winston Cup circuit, until legislation changed that." She shrugged. "It's just an interesting connection."

Alton was a short, stout man and since Tatum was over six feet tall without an inch of fat, Alton often teased Evelyn, "You sure he's mine, right?"

Her face would redden and in a stern voice, she would say, "Alton, that old joke was not funny before and it certainly isn't now." He sat down on a chair for visitors, resting the toes of his shoes on the floor as he tilted the chair back.

"As best I recall, the story went something like this: Howard was forced to sell Sapelo because he didn't have enough money to finish building the Cloister here on Sea Island. The Depression had arrived in a shabby style so many people, including millionaires like Howard Coffin, were suffering. Broke his heart, though, and he never recovered. He loved Sapelo. Have you seen it?"

"No. Pepper and I are going over tomorrow to meet the Sheriff there. The Governor is coming, too. You heard about Mrs. Puckett's nephew? He's being accused of a murder at the Big House, whatever that is."

Alton, stroking his chin, looked out as a couple of people rode by on bicycles. "That would be the Reynolds Mansion.

84

The Georgia Department of Natural Resources bought the house and most of the island. They rent it out for group conferences, things like that. The other day, I was coming back from a lunch with Bill and Ginger Hodges who live on Sapelo—oh my, can that woman cook—and as I was getting off the ferry, a dozen or so people in a wedding party were getting on. I figured they were going to the Reynolds House because where else would they be staying? There wasn't another ferry leaving until the next day."

Alton, a master of real estate statistics, liked to be precise about property. "Now, I'm no expert on the Reynolds House. I know much more about Musgrove, the Reynolds' plantation here on St. Simons. But if I'm not mistaken, it was Thomas Spalding who built the original house long before the Civil War. After Spalding died, the house spent 50 or 60 years just falling apart. Seems to me that some group up in Macon worked on rebuilding it some, and taking away all the foliage that covered it. Coffin used to bring new cars down to Savannah in the winter months to test them. Then he started racing them against each other and maybe Ford and other manufacturers. Henry Ford had a plantation near Savannah, too. Around 1912, near the time the Titanic sank and that's why I remember, Coffin bought the entire island, rebuilt the house by reinforcing the tabby with stucco, then added a second floor. He and his wife loved it a great deal. When Reynolds bought it, he spent additional money on it." He pointed to a photo on the wall. "That's Darien."

Stella nodded. She loved the little fishing village that was just a few miles across the water from Sapelo. Recently, a new hotel named The Oaks on the River had been built there. She and Marlo had been over to appraise a house recently, so they had a lovely, early dinner at the hotel, watching as fishing boats returned from a day's work. Nothing fancy about the little town but it sure had a lot of personality.

"When I was in sports marketing, I was in the Winston-Salem area a lot," Stella responded. "R.J. Reynolds, Sr. married later in life. I think his oldest son, R.J.R, Jr. was in his mid-twenties or so when his father died, and he came into an enormous fortune."

"Young lady, I believe you're right about all that. Junior was an early believer in aviation. Even knew the Wright brothers. He seeded the money for a couple of airlines, too. Perhaps Eastern and Delta, both." He suddenly hopped up from his chair. "Well, there's money out there, just waiting for me to pick it up, so I've got to get at it. I have to show a property at the north end of the island." He drained his coffee cup, called out a goodbye to Marlo, who had returned to her office, but when he got to the door, he stopped and turned back. "Hey, Stellie, I don't know if this is the gospel or not but my Daddy used to say that when Howard gathered all the investors together to start a new car company, they decided to name it after Mr. Hudson. Since motor cars, as they were called then, were only a few years old, they were afraid they couldn't sell one called a Coffin!" He threw back his bald head and laughed uproariously, still chuckling as he walked to his car.

Chapter Six

☙

"Are you still with me?" Jackson Culpepper said over the telephone.

Stella snapped back to reality after a very long moment in her past. "Oh, Pepper, I'm sorry. I was thinking of the research I did about Sapelo yesterday. I didn't have time to tell you because Chatty demands so much attention. And then we were at the Burnetts'. I'll tell you about it on the ride to ferry. It's pretty interesting, historically."

"Sounds good. I'll pick you up in about 40 minutes. Now, listen: be ready because ferries don't wait for Marshals or pretty women."

The Governor had already told them that he would meet them at the ferry because he wanted to stop in Darien and talk to the Sheriff's office investigator privately. The one who had been first on the scene.

"I'll be ready. I promise. See you then." She replaced the receiver and had taken less than three steps when the phone rang again. She laughed, thinking Pepper was calling back.

"Hey, you," she said after picking up the receiver.

"Mrs. Bankwell?" asked a deep voice with a British accent. She knew immediately who it was. Chatty's Sea Island butler, Bailey. He had a different British butler in Atlanta. Chatty often affectionately called him, "Baileywick".

"Bailey, I'm sorry," she said. "I thought it was a friend I'd just talked with."

"Yes ma'am, I understand. I beg your pardon for the earliness of the hour."

Stella laughed. "Bailey, surely you know by now that Chatham does not mind what time it is as long as he gets what he wants. And I'm sure he instructed you to call."

No well-trained British butler, a 'gentleman's gentleman' as Chatty was fond of saying, would ever participate in such dialogue. Stella knew it but she had to have her own laugh.

"Mr. Colquitt requests that you wait for him at your house this morning, ma'am, because he will be joining you on the trip to Sapelo."

Stella almost dropped the phone. "What? Bailey, am I to understand that you're saying that Mr. Colquitt's coming with us?"

"That is correct, ma'am."

"Does Mr. Colquitt realize that this is probably an overnight trip? On an untamed island? Bailey, there is no china or silver on Sapelo."

"Correct, ma'am. I'm friends with Stacy Row in the traveler's center and he escorted me over there once. I agree that it is no place for a gentleman, but Mr. Colquitt insists. I have explained it is, shall we say, 'primitive'?"

"Yes!" exclaimed Stella. "That's it—primitive. And not even fashionably primitive like Grandma Moses. This is the likes of which Chatty has never seen in his whole, entitled life." Truth be told, Stella Bankwell had never been to the island, but she was well apprised of what was needed: sturdy clothes, shoes, a hat, a flashlight, no jewelry other than her watch, a pair of good gardening gloves, and bug spray though it was speculated to be too early for the bugs. Stella was stunned. One thing she did know from experience: trying to talk Chatty out of this was worthless. She'd just lose time and miss the ferry. He'd have to find out for himself. Stella looked at the clock.

"Bailey, please, have Mr. Colquitt at my house in 34 minutes. *34 minutes.*" This felt like a good time to use Colquitt's beloved italics. "Bailey, please, you can't be late or we will miss the ferry and I will be in trouble with everyone. As much as I love him, I'll have to leave him behind."

"Yes, ma'am, I understand the gravity of the situation."

"And your employer does realize this is an overnight trip?"

"Apparently, he does, ma'am. In fact, he instructed me to prepare a valise for him."

Stella rolled her eyes. "Well, be certain to put in his nicest silk pajamas and a robe," she replied, sarcastically. She knew, of course, that Bailey, being British, wouldn't get the sarcasm and Chatty would choose some custom-made pajamas that came from Paris or London. She was just about to hang up when she remembered, "Oh, Bailey, Mr. Colquitt will need a hamper of food and drinks. There are no stores or accommodations on the island."

"I understand," he replied. "We won't be late."

Stella hung up the phone. "A valise and a hamper? Typical Chatty." She looked at the clock again and jumped. She made sure that Spigot had water and food then jumped in and out of the shower. Owing to a tradition going back to childhood, she laid out her clothes every night. Thank goodness. Dashing on her make-up, she dressed quickly in cotton, orange and pink floral slacks paired with an orange sweater, pulled on a hat, sunglasses, and grabbed a light coat out of the closet. She had just enough time for a spritz of perfume, a couple of minutes with Spigot, and a call to Marlo, reminding her that she was babysitting that day and night. Then, Stella stepped out the door, the gentle sun already warming the day. She sat on the front porch swing, enjoying the breeze from the other side of Beachview, and waited for Pepper. She looked at a bush of blooming azaleas in hot pink. It had been her first time to sit and ponder the dashing Marshal since the night when he'd tried to kiss her.

Stella shook her head, thinking back to the Burnetts' terrace. She wanted to kiss him so much. Her heart was thumping—but then Mrs. Puckett interrupted them with the news about Campbell Puckett and that's pretty much all she had thought of it since then.

"If it's meant to be, it will happen," Mama used to say. Stella hated those words. It was like something Walt Disney would have Mickey say to Minnie. It took a long time in life for Stella to learn patience, but she had more now than ever. Still, she wouldn't be comfortable without knowing the plan or when it might happen. Her Mama was right. Nothing could stand between what should happen and what shouldn't. Seeing Spigot's face, looking out the window with the curtain pushed back, she smiled. She hadn't had a dog in years but Spigot was worth waiting on. If she could wait on the right dog (though she wasn't looking for a dog) then she could wait on the right man. And who knew? If not Pepper, then maybe the real Prince would come today. Just so long as he wasn't another wrong one like Asher Bankwell, she was willing to wait.

She heard the large, heavy, dark sedan turn the corner on to her street and watched as it pulled in behind her SUV. It was, of course, tall, handsome, grinning Jackson "Pepper" Culpepper. For a quick second, she thought how funny it was that her maiden name of Jackson was the same as Pepper's first name. When the two of them had stumbled into each other at the King and Prince and figured that out, they were, at first stunned, then laughed at the preposterous joke.

"Hello, my gorgeous sleuth." He saw a picnic basket and a hearty tapestry overnight zippered bag with a black background and respectful (not silly) flowers decorating it. All would have to admit that it, indeed, looked durable for an "un-groomed" island.

Stella got out of the swing and walked over to Pepper as he took her hand and helped her down the steps. "Looks like you've packed wise."

"I hope so. An extra set of clothes, sweats for warmth and the night." She stopped and made a very funny face. "And very sexy, too." Pepper's heart sputtered for just a moment, then she winked and laughed. "Who needs sexy on Sapelo, right?"

"Huh, yeah, I guess. It looks like the Gullah Geechees did fine without them. They raised families up nicely." Pepper was putting the bag and basket in the truck. When they got to the ferry, they would have to leave the car behind. McCager, only he could do it, had a friend there named Bill who owned a couple cottages for family visits so he had assured the Governor that they would have their cottages.

"Fine, fine man that Bill—and here's the thing. He is smarter than the whole state of Georgia because he knows a little bit about everything," The Governor had said to Miss Alva the previous day, after Bill Raymond had come over following the murder, and explained the lay of the land.

The Gullahs were former slaves who now lived on a couple of hundred acres of the island with their village, church, and friendships. Most of them weren't likely to take in any new friends, particularly a federal officer, a fair-haired maiden, and crusty old McCager. Mainly, they just wanted to be left alone. But they did enjoy what the federal or state government could provide for them such as high-speed Internet and phone service.

In Stella's research, stories varied. Some, old enough to remember, loved Mr. Reynolds while others would have preferred to build their houses with stones, themselves, without his help. They weren't afraid of anybody or anything. Not even the wild alligators, rattle snakes, or the feral cows. As far as the Gullahs and animals were concerned, Sapelo was their island. Even though it was a tourism spot for the DNR, the Gullahs didn't much care to have folks around.

Just as Pepper slammed the truck lid on the standard issue vehicle for the US Marshals, he walked around the passenger's side, opened the door for Stella, and said, "Your carriage. I'm sorry I couldn't get an expensive SUV, but this is comfortable, has new tires, the radio works, and it is glistening with clean." He bowed his head. "Your humble servant."

Stella smiled and replied flirtatiously. "Why, Marshal, I didn't realize we had a date today."

He touched his forehead as a salute and said, "Any day with you feels like a date." Yes, Pepper was going to be absolutely professional because this was a murder as well as a possible tragedy that could destroy the life of a young man with such a bright future. "But don't worry, Ms. Bankwell, I will be just another US Marshal, admiring a lovely woman from afar." Then, in a lowered timbre of voice, he added, "I just want to make sure you're safe." They both stopped and looked at each other, he was thinking of kissing her when his "specially trained" super awareness alerted him that a car was approaching toward them a bit fast.

"Stella, get in and lock it," he said and practically pushed her inside.

On the oversized vehicle—used mostly by drug mobs and folks with too much money—as it pulled up, the left door was opened by a man. Pepper unsnapped the clasp across the Glock in its holster. He couldn't see the man's head as it bobbed up and down, retrieving things off the floor, then stretching toward something in back.

The driver opened his door to help. "Oh, great," Pepper thought to himself. "Just what I did not need—Chatty."

Chatty emerged from the vehicle, looking as if he were the master of the hunt: dressed in a tweed riding jacket with suede patches on the elbows, matching vest, a lightweight turtleneck, jodhpurs (like the ones worn by professional horse riders), riding boots that stretched to his knees, and a matching tweed, billed driving cap.

For a couple of seconds, Pepper stood akimbo, shaking his head.

"Chatty, are you headed to a steeplechase?" Pepper called, trying to bat down the extreme irritation he felt. Again, Chatty had intruded on some badly needed private time for him with Stella.

Chatty proudly stood up and straightened his vest and jacket. "How do I look, Pepper?" he asked smiling from ear to ear. "I hope I look as good as I feel because I feel great today. Going on this tremendous adventure with y'all and the Governor is just too good."

Pepper was still trying to get his head around *why* Chatty was going. It had not been mentioned last night while they were at the Burnetts' and Stella said nothing about it on the phone. Bailey, meanwhile, was asking permission to place two large, wood-weaved hampers in the car as well as Chatty's elegant valise.

"Look!" Chatty said excitedly. "I have a tiny horse whip to protect against the animals of the island. The big one looked more cowboy and didn't match this outfit, I didn't think. Where's Stella? I need to ask her."

Pepper put his hand against Chatty's shoulder and asked, "Did she invite you?"

Chatty looked a little hurt then tossed off the pain quickly. "No, but Bailey called this morning and ascertained that everything would be alright. She told Bailey to make sure that I brought my best custom-made silk pajamas. And I did," he finished in his singsong voice. Pepper no longer felt disappointment. Inside, he was chuckling because he knew that Stella had not been deliberately mean. The pajamas were a joke, but Bailey was English and didn't get the joke, and Chatty would believe that Bailey had everything correct.

Pepper patted the top of the car, "We need to get going or we'll miss the ferry." Chatty was trying to push the hampers aside, to get his husky body pried inside.

Stella looked over her shoulder. "Well, you did come after all." Disgruntled, Pepper fastened his seatbelt and put the car into gear.

"Yes!" he sang out. "I was terribly troubled last time that you might not be safe so I wanted to be there."

Under his sunglasses, which accentuated his jawline, Pepper rolled his eyes and pulled the car onto Beachview Drive. "Well, Secretariat, we're glad to have you."

Chatty's well-hatted head popped up from the back seat. "Secretariat was a horse. What are you saying?" He took his little whip and tapped Pepper on the shoulder, "Don't you be mean, Jackson Culpepper. We have to play well together to solve this murder."

Like a child, Chatty looked back at Bailey standing stick straight, waiting until the car with his master, pulled away. Chatty, like a kid headed for his favorite play camp, smiled happily while waving goodbye, enthusiastically, from the heavily-tinted rear window to the boy left behind.

Watching Chatty in the review mirror, Pepper looked sideways at Stella and said, "This is either going to be a great story or a bad memory. I'm not sure which.

Chapter Seven

❧

The four friends strolled down the ferry gangplank and three of them were wide-eyed at the primitive, natural beauty.

Governor Burnett had been there many times so he was no stranger to the ocean vista and live oaks hanging heavy with moss. If pressed, he would probably have to admit that it was his favorite island of the fourteen islands off the Georgia coast. He and Miss Alva had spent many nights at the Reynolds House. In fact, whenever he had an important speech to prepare, it was almost a sure bet that he would be huddled up in the Reynolds House. Once, when he was Governor, he had even had a family reunion for the Burnetts there. They were shuttled over in two ferries then enjoyed a catered picnic. Cager laughed to himself whenever he remembered overhearing one of his bewildered aunts ask another, "Did you know that McCager had *this* much power?"

The house was pretty much as it was in 1964 when the junior Reynolds had died. That was one thing McCager Burnett loved about it—the smell of yesterday and times gone by. Tobacco money was enormous in the first eighty years of the century, before the health hazards had been unearthed, but the scion, to whom so much money had come from the huge tobacco company, would not live to see the slowdown in revenue.

On the ferry ride over, three of them had discussed the murder while one of them had let the wind blow through his hair in a princely fashion, preoccupied with the lint on his riding pants.

Just over forty-eight hours before, Spencer Houghton, a pharmaceutical executive and heir, was found in a heap of death at the bottom of the steps leading from the kitchen to the basement. At first glance, it looked like too much wine at a corporate party had resulted in a stumble down the stairs. And, so it would have been filed away as "accidental death" at the age of sixty-three—except for an eager, young medical student in the medical examiner's office.

The victim's neck was broken, for certain, while the experts declared (after a dozen interviews revealed how much he'd had to drink) that he had opened the door by mistake, one he thought would lead into a bathroom but, instead, was a steep staircase; one that would lead to his death. No one had actually seen it happen.

Joseph Maycomb was from the poorest-of-the-poor in the practically starving town of Sparta, Georgia. This was a town where much of the main street was boarded up, yet an enormous effort had restored the crumbling courthouse before, and again after, a devastating fire raged then sputtered on and off for three weeks. It was a setback for the tiny town that had just lifted its head off the "Places in Peril" list. But Joseph Maycomb came from people that didn't just lay down and take it. His family and others worked for two years to restore the courthouse to such magnificence that it became known as "Her Majesty" around Hancock County and glistened with such beauty that it took one's eyes off the crumbling town.

It wasn't hard to be the valedictorian of his high school class—most students were grateful just to graduate and would take on living hard like the generations before—but it was tough to be in the top five at Emory Medical school which is where he landed thanks to scholarships and parents who worked multiple jobs. His father, Hank, ran a farm for a high-faluting man who lived in Atlanta while his mother, Ocie, worked in the high school lunchroom as well as at a second job at a run-down convenience store. She was tough and had escaped at least a dozen hold-ups and had, once, even wrestled a gun away from a drunk dope dealer. He had to be drunk to take on Miss Ocie because the rest of the town knew better.

Joseph had been brought up to seek help on his bended knee and to always stand tall and be proud of who he was and from whence he came. The 911 call was received just after midnight, so the Department of Natural Resources arranged an emergency boat from Darien to Sapelo. On the ride over, the law officials had discussed whether anyone had ever been murdered on Sapelo. It was a peaceful, neighborly place, anchored by Hog Hammock, a community of Gullah Geechees, descendants of enslaved West African people, brought to the island in the 1700s to work on the plantations.

They had survived the Civil War and now just wanted to survive modern day life and the teasing of money brought in by people blessed enough to build sweet, modest homes overlooking the glistening, pristine beaches. The Gullah Geechees knew how to take care of their own and survive happily doing it. On the weekends, the ferry was heavy with islanders hitching a ride over to Darien for groceries, then back that afternoon. School children caught the ferry at seven o'clock every morning and landed in Darien at 7:30 a.m. to an awaiting school bus. It would be close to 4:30 p.m. before they slammed the screen doors behind them, coming home, so an education was hard-earned for the Gullah Geechees. But so far, many had survived the grueling pace required for schooling—including one of their own who had made it to the highest ranks of professional football.

On the slow ride over in the post-midnight hour, as they shined lights across the dark water and felt their way, minute by minute, one of the oldest men on the boat opined that he was certain there had been a murder in long years past, but he couldn't rightly recall any details. Besides, reminded a law officer who was among the passengers, right now, this was a death call. Nobody had said anything about "murder."

Yet.

Most probably, it would have gone unnoticed as anything other than a drunken mishap except that Joseph Maycomb kept studying the body and how it had fallen. He wasn't convinced that it was a stumble but was, instead, a full force push down the stairs. He pressed the issue with his supervisor, arguing that if the body had tumbled down, it most likely wouldn't have had that hard hit of a cement beam across the victim's forehead. Joseph had been fortunate enough that, when the call came in, he was able to scramble out of the bunkbed in his basement apartment and make it to the dock in time to catch the ferry over to Sapelo.

Perhaps, if there had been more "unnatural deaths" on Sapelo in the middle of the night, authorities would have been more organized and so a medical student wouldn't have made it aboard the first boat out. But as it happened, for all involved, Joseph was a hungry soul, looking for a break and a life far away from Sparta.

With the death of Spencer Marcus Houghton, working heir to one of America's most prosperous families, a poor kid from one of Sparta's finest families was on his way to notable success.

Chapter Eight

ଔ

"But, sir, excuse me. It just doesn't add up." Joseph May-comb was raised to be stubborn, hard-working and, always, courteous. It was easy enough to say a six-foot-tall-man had stumbled, drunkenly, down the stairs but it was the broad mark across his forehead that was sticking in his craw.

His supervisor was in no mood to be questioned. It was almost noon and he had been up most of the night. He just wanted a good meal, a hot shower, and warm bed. The supervisor, Theodore, heaved a weary sigh. He had spent weeks putting up with the overeager student, Joseph, who questioned every move in the small office.

"Do you want to run this office and let *me* go back to medical school?" he growled to Joseph.

"No, sir. I don't mean to disrespect you. My Mama would whup my tail if I did that." Joseph paused for a moment. Hancock County, where he was raised, was about ninety percent African American. In Sparta, they all knew how to deal with each other so his primary education, outside of Emory, was how to stand his ground without being disrespectful. Joseph picked up the chart and started across the room. He turned back around to try it from a different approach when Theodore—who Joseph had nicknamed "Mr. Rascal," even to his face—walked over and put his arm around the kind-hearted student.

"Joseph, I'm sorry. I'm just a grouchy, old man." He grinned as he took his glasses off and rubbed his eyes. "That's why you nicknamed me 'Mr. Rascal,' right?" Joseph chuckled and nodded. Theodore meant well and had always been thoughtful. Although he was only a year away from retirement and could have glided through the last few years, Theodore always strived to do his best to invest in the students that came his way. He ran his hands through his silvering hair and tried to explain, again, especially since Joseph was not showing any signs of caving.

"Joe," he began. He wasn't the only person who had ever shortened his name to Joe, but it was befitting. It sounded right when it came from the old Rascal. "I worry that you're lookin' for a big break to come from a little ol' place like this. I've been at this job for many a'moon and I've never seen a murder on Sapelo. They wanna be left alone and they leave others alone. Now, what are the odds that you're a student and you run into a big case before you're even outta school? In a place with no crime. Think about it like that."

Joseph, who was six feet tall and weighed less than a hundred and forty pounds, hitched up his britches as he nodded. "Yes, sir. When you look at it that way, I guess it does sound right."

Theodore smiled warmly, patted him on the back and said, "I'm goin' home for a few hours of shut-eye. You can go home, too, or catch a few zzz's on the sofa in my office. Just don't worry yourself to death." He laughed wearily. "I promise that life will give you plenty of chances to worry." He took the young man by the shoulders and looked him straight in the eye. "When I was a young whippersnapper, I thought I could solve the world's problems. Before I knew it, life had kicked me to the ground. First, I pinched pennies to save up to get married. Then, we'd live on Campbell's soup for a week, just to make a car payment. Next thing we knew, a baby was on the way. It's been a rollercoaster ride ever since. Now, I'll tell you what's what—worrying yourself over a baby, thinking she has a fatal disease when it's a minor cold. Those are the things worth worrying over. Not a rich man, on a fancy corporate retreat, who got drunk and fell down a set of basement stairs."

Again, Joseph nodded because Mr. Rascal made a lot of sense. He had grown up with a family full of level-headed thinkers. His Grandpaw, Odom, used to sit on the front porch of his tiny house and wait for people to come by and ask for advice. He was happy to oblige, too. He'd give them a glass of cold spring water in a mason jar and the talk would begin. People stopped by the little house, coming in and out of his Grandpappy's, for therapy sessions that might last all afternoon and into nightfall. Every person who stopped by said that they left feeling better about their self and the world. At their little Baptist church that set far off the road, amidst a thunder of tall Georgia pines, people called him "Solomon" more often than they called him Odom. If anyone ever questioned his wisdom after he had carefully laid out the answer, he'd say, "Well, okay, let's look at another way. If two women brung you a baby, a'claimin' to be the Mama, would you give up the baby or divide him in half?"

Joseph's people were all Bible thinkers. They knew the Bible up one side and down the other and what you, quite rightly, didn't want to do was bring them anything other than a King James Bible. So, if old Solomon brought up a Bible story of any kind, they were liable to back down. As a toddler, Joseph had often heard his Mama and Aunts talk about how his Grandpappy learned himself to read, just so he could read the Bible.

"Now, that right there's a fact," said his Aunt Eunice. "He used to have my Mama read the scriptures over and over to him until they thought he was recitin' 'stead of readin' when he was four. When I's just a youngin', Daddy used to say 'People learn through stories. That's how Jesus taught. People kin call 'em parables all day long but I say that they're stories. Plain and simple.'"

Ol' man Odom "Solomon" Maycomb never had a more devoted disciple than Joseph. He had hung on every word his Grandpappy ever said. Now, it had come down from Sparta in the last week that his beloved Grandpappy was drawing nigh toward his death. Joseph didn't want his hero to leave this "ol 'vale of tears and sorrows" as his Grandpappy called it, without making him proud.

"Now, son, someday, I'll be on the other side of the mighty River Jordan, where I believe the good Lord, some time or 'nother, will pull back the veil to let me see how you is doin' down here. Make me proud. Mighty proud. I'm a-countin' on you." The old man looked down at the red dirt clay under his feet, scratching it with the cane that he had recently taken to carrying. He had spent 15 years, carving on the cane, the wood beautiful, yellow Cyprus pulled from the center of a log.

Those words stayed in Joseph's mind. They haunted him. Now, he wondered if he wasn't trying to outdo Jesus and make his Grandpappy proud before his home-going. Joseph smiled, thinking to himself, "I should be thinking of the peace that he's about to attain and the great glory he'll see"— but, selfishly, he couldn't. Then, again, to himself, he said, "Justice must be done for Spencer Houghton. No one else. That's who I have to focus on."

Mr. Rascal had gone to his office to put away a file. Now, he came back to find Joseph standing at his tiny, corner desk, still holding the Spencer Houghton file in his hand. He was staring down at the old out-of-style linoleum floor, deep in thought. Rascal waited a minute before jarring Joseph out of his dream world.

"Son," he said gently. "Don't make me turn the lights out on you. You might get stuck in the vault when you put up that file."

Joseph looked up and smiled. "Yes, sir."

The Rascal chuckled. "Did I ever tell you the story about the intern who got locked in that vault?"

Joseph shook his head. They had a small vault in their office where they kept six filing cabinets and a couple of chairs. The door swung closed, automatically, and locked until 8 a.m. the next morning.

"I declare on my life that he fell asleep in there. He was the lazy type. He could fall asleep at the drop of a hat. It's not a fun over-the-night stay. Or so's been told to me. I was away on vacation when it happened, but they told me that he was beside himself the next morning. I think he still has anxiety from it. When the vault is closed, it doesn't open until the timer opens it the next morning. No other way." He chuckled about it and recounting a similar story of the medical examiner who, once, while working on loan-out from Nashville after a major hurricane, had met such a misfortune in Brunswick."

"Why was he in there?" Joseph asked. He thought back instantly to a tragedy in Sparta years before when a young boy, playing out in the woods, discovered an old refrigerator he'd climbed inside, thinking it would be a special, secret place to hide. It took the community several days to find him. Joseph shook his head at the memory of the boy's mother's cries and howls.

Joseph had slipped into his own world again before Mr. Rascal had time to answer.

"Daydreamer, huh?" Rascal mumbled, shrugged then rolled up the paper sack in which his wife had sent three ham and cheese sandwiches that morning when he had gotten the emergency call. Mr. Rascal's wife, Miss Joyce, knew food was hard to find on the island unless someone took you in to feed you. Wordlessly, she'd stepped out of bed, grabbed her robe from the hook in the bathroom, and headed to the kitchen. Yeah, there weren't many "after midnight" calls for Sapelo so she was both curious and dutiful. But she wanted to make sure her husband was fed.

"Do you know what happened?" she asked.

"No. Just a death at the Reynolds House. They found him at the bottom of the stairs."

She nodded and said, "Give me a second to make sandwiches. I'll be quick." True to her word, the sandwiches and two bottles of water were ready by the time Theodore had his clothes on and had dug out his waterproof boots.

Before leaving the office, he had started to toss the bag in the nearby trash can and stopped. Why throw away a perfectly good sack that could be used again? That's how Miss Joyce and he had lived in their young years: they washed zip lock bags, turning them inside-out to dry. Mr. Rascal had even often seen his wife take a barely used paper towel, rinse it out, and lay it by the sink to dry so she could use it again.

As he pulled on the same gray jacket he had been wearing for 20 years, he reminded Joseph, "Remember, don't let the lights get turned out on you. Go home and get some sleep. Likely as not, we'll have to go back somewhere in the next 24 hours looking for anything we might've missed. By the way. Ol' McCager Burnett is bringing a US Marshal and couple of tourists or whatever they are, with him. Not sure why they are comin'."

Joking, he flipped the lights off, then on again, and that got Joseph's attention, who looked up quickly from the file.

Theodore grinned and threw him a wave. "Get going," he said over his shoulder.

"Yes, sir! Right away, I'm going."

Only he wasn't.

Chapter Nine

❦

A white DNR truck, with lettering on the side, and an orange Kuboto ATV, about the size of a small truck, with large, go-anywhere tires, was waiting for the foursome when they crossed the gangplank into the parking area.

Chatty was busy, looking about at the gorgeous views, when his eye was caught by the white sand roads. He then looked down at his Jimmy Choo Nell leather riding boots in black. With his kind of money, $2,000 wasn't much for foot-wear—but he hated to be dusty and for his boots to be dirty. The other three paid no attention to his dilemma.

"All aboard," the Governor announced, opening the truck's passenger door.

"Governor, if the authorities have already decided this was an accident caused by too much alcohol, why are we here?" asked Chatty, suddenly breaking from his reverie. "And why would they have arrested Mrs. Puckett's nephew?"

"First of all, the death certificate hasn't been signed off on," he replied." Until then, it's still an open case. Secondly, the Houghtons are a wildly rich and influential family. Spencer's father is eighty-six and still very much alive. He doesn't want his family's legacy to include a drunk who died by falling down a set of stairs."

"Well, that's understandable. But why would Campbell Puckett have been arrested?" Chatty asked.

"The Sheriff's investigator told me that the gardener said he saw Houghton and Campbell having an argument on the front lawn, earlier in the day. Campbell told me that he and Houghton were just having a fun conversation. That it was animated conversation about wildlife and the size of fish." The Governor fell into a quiet moment as the others were gathering their things and climbing into the vehicles. "The oddest thing happened while I was in the Sheriff's office this morning—Atlanta's most expensive defense attorney called and said he had been retained to help with Campbell's defense." McCager shook his head. "It doesn't make sense. I and the other attorney in our office are representing him pro bono. I don't know where this other lawyer would have come from."

"Excuse me—"

"What is it now?" the Governor asked, growing somewhat annoyed by all of Chatty's sudden questions.

"This is important, Governor. What about my boots?"

The three of them looked at Chatty's dusty boots then back up, at Chatty, in disbelief.

"Chatty. Really?" Stella asked.

He was bewildered. "What?"

CR

The Governor was in no mood to be tested. He'd had little sleep in the past two days. It had started with an early morning call a day earlier from the Governor of Mississippi after Spencer Houghton's brother had called him on behalf of his father and family. Very quickly, Cager learned that the Houghtons had been among the biggest contributors to the Governor's campaign because they were Mississippi born and still kept their corporate offices there as well as a small plant.

"Cagey," Governor Bill Alverson began, using the nickname that went back to when they had served in Congress together, then later as fellow Governors in Georgia and Mississippi. Too, they were both Southerners so they understood each well. Almost always, they had been allies though they had taken a different stance on an extra ten cent taxation on milk. Burnett came from Georgia where dairy was an important commodity. Finally, the two men agreed by swapping votes. Burnett would vote for cotton replanting after a tornado had torn up a good bit of Yazoo and much of the Delta while Governor Alverson would vote against the milk taxation.

"You only call me 'Cagey' when you're up to no good," Burnett said, half-teasing, half-joking. "You're lucky that I'm an early riser. I'd be in a real bad mood if you had woken me up."

"I'm not teasing this time. I'm in a fix. You've been a Governor and you know how these rich people can be."

"Yeah, I do. My sympathies to you," Burnett laughed. "But then again, Georgia's got a whole lot more millionaires than Mississippi. That means I had a lot more problems than you."

William Mason Alverson was tall, skinny, had hair the color of an orange, and freckles that spread across his face making him look thirty-five when he was over sixty. He could be grouchy but so could every Governor, yet most of the time, he was kind and friendly to all who knew him.

"Why's this such an aggravation?" asked McCager.

"Ever heard of Malachi Pharmaceuticals?" he asked.

McCager thought for a moment. Malachi was the name of a book in the Old Testament but there was something else about it. "Wait, give me a second. I read something recently about it somewhere." The paper he read most often was the *Wall Street Journal*. He'd rather know financial news than how fellow politicians were being torpedoed. "Oh, wait a minute! It's that company with the new weight loss drug that so many people are using." He started laughing. "I read a quote from a woman the other day that said it's the best drug since the birth control pill. In fact, according to this woman, it's better."

Alverson laughed. "That company has made a lot of money and paid a lot of Mississippi taxes. I'm beholdin' to that family on many accounts. The old man practically funded my entire first political race. Chairman of the County Commission. He was mad at the other one for some long-forgotten reason. That company is over one hundred and thirty years old. They specialize in over-the-counter drugs with the exception of this new diet fad. Do you remember Tylan Two Way Cold Tablets?"

"As a matter of a fact, I do," Cage replied. "My old Grandpaw, up in the mountains, used to buy it when he could afford it—a nickle a pack."

"Mine, too." Alverson admitted. "Well, that's how they got their start. Used to advertise on the Grand Ole Opry with Martha White and other products."

"Folks don't realize what good advertisin' the Grand Ole Opry gave products to people, particularly."

"Well, the Malachi company got their start with those cold tablets. A little later, they had a tonic that fixed just about anything that needed fixin'. That's because it had a little-known drug in it named opium, with a tiny bit of cocaine, too. It came in a small bottle and was flavored where it tasted real good. Made people feel real good, too. That lasted a number of years before it got taken off the market following several deaths."

Cager Burnett was a sensible person so he had quite a few questions. "Billy," Cage began, addressing Alverson by his nickname that was used only by close friends, "Are they incorporated in Mississippi?"

"Delaware. That's where a lot of old companies are incorporated because of the corporate-friendly environment. But now, in all fairness, the company was founded down here, around Greenwood, and they still employ about three-hundred Mississippians." All of a sudden, a thought hit him.

"Do you know that Bobbie Gentry, who wrote *Ode to Billy Joe*, is from Greenwood?"

"You don't say."

"And she wrote 'Fancy,' too.'" Alverson was on a roll. "Fred Carl who started the Viking Range company is from there, too."

"Mississippi is a lot bigger than I give y'all credit for," he said with a laugh. "We've established that the Houghtons have a lot of money and they threw you into politics. Why do you need my help? I'm retired from politics, enjoying the good life on Sea Island, that is: I'm enjoying it when I don't have to go to Atlanta and work."

"Sapelo Island," Alverson said.

"Most beautiful place you've never seen."

"One of the Houghtons was killed over there last night."

McCager Burnett sat straight up in his chair. "Mrs. Puckett!"

"Who?" asked the puzzled Alverson.

"Our housekeeper. Been with us over thirty years. We were having a dinner party last night. She was finishing the cleaning of the kitchen when she got a call that her nephew had been arrested for a murder on Sapelo."

"Have many murders happened on Sapelo?" the Mississippi Governor asked.

"First one I ever heard of. And how do you even know it was a murder? Was he shot?"

"I don't know."

"Stabbed?"

"I don't know about that."

"Alverson, what *do* you know? Maybe that'll make it easier on you."

"Spencer Marcus Houghton, the oldest son, was found dead at the foot of the steps leading down into the basement."

"He could have fallen," McCager replied sensibly.

"Maybe. But the family is resisting that notion. His blood alcohol level was pretty high."

"He wouldn't be the first drunk to fall down a flight of stairs."

"Colorado Houghton—that's the father's name, who was named after his great-grandfather who unearthed copper in the wild West, adding to the early Houghton wealth—is pretty upset. Not just over losing his son but the scandal it will be." Governor Alverson said. "He and the family have had enough scandal. A daughter killed in a car wreck with a husband who wasn't her own. A son, somewhere along the line, died from drugs, and another Houghton, back in the 1920s, had a complete mental breakdown and never again saw the outside of an asylum."

Cager picked up his favorite pipe, laying on the desk, and studied it. He was sitting in his office, in a deep red leather swivel chair, where he leaned back and put his feet on his desk. It wasn't something he did often, Miss Alva frowned on it mightily, but he was in stocking feet so how much could it hurt?

"Well, first of all, rich or not, you can't just go around, having a young man with a mighty clean record as a hard worker and servant of the Almighty, arrested. Secondly, the Houghtons don't pay taxes in Georgia so I'm not particularly worried about that. I'm worried about Campbell Puckett. So, they think that railroading a young man is better than a rich one falling down the stairs, drunk?"

"Absolutely," the answer was quick. "That would be someone else's fault."

Cage's mind wandered back to his first visit to Sapelo. He was a twelve-year-old Boy Scout. It had been a big adventure to travel old roads, long before the Interstates, and it was a long way from Turniptown. It was on that trip when McCager saw the ocean for the first time and there was no prettier place to see it than during a ferry ride from Darien to Sapelo. If he were to admit it as an aging man now, he'd have to tell how spooky the island was with its huge trees, hanging moss, old houses—most belonging to the Gullah Geechees—swamps, and the most gorgeous stretch of beach that, to this day, was the most beautiful that Cage had ever seen.

Thoughtfully, he said, "To be honest, I'd hate to admit that a murder happened on Sapelo. Miss Alva and I used to take our niece and two nephews over there. We'd stay in the Reynolds House. There was no television and barely a radio signal, so the kids would run and whoop it up, outside. We'd bring our groceries so Miss Alva cooked for us, then we played Monopoly or Trivial Pursuit. One year, the Chamber of Commerce made up a gift of Georgia trivia to give to its members. To this day, those kids all say they know more about this state, from that game, than from any history book."

Alverson had never visited Sapelo, but he had heard tales and they were all lovely. "Was Reynolds still alive when you were there as a Boy Scout?"

For a moment, Cage thought of Reynolds and how he had taken the time to show special birds to the boys and to explain different kinds of fish. Among the many reasons Reynolds so loved Sapelo was the tremendous variation of fish, fowl, and other wildlife. They lived in abundance on the island, and it was also one of the reasons that Howard Coffin adored the place, as well.

There was a storied legend that Coffin and his beloved nephew Alfred "Bill" Jones, Sr. once decided to see how many nights their cook could make dinner from different varieties of food on the island. The estimate was decided—between fish, fowl, and other wildlife—to be between 35 to 50, depending on who told the story. Whatever the number, it was impressive and agreed by all, that it was a story to be passed down through the ages.

Once, an alligator had sneaked up on Reynolds from behind. This was a tale that a little boy named Cage had spent most of his life "a'tellin'" as he liked to say. The boys saw it but couldn't make a sound come out of their mouths. They pointed, then turned and ran. When Reynolds saw it behind him, he grabbed a nearby, sizable log and knocked the heck out of the gator's jaw. Then he hurried—he did not run—

away. It was a lesson that struck with McCager Burnett—always stay cool and never run away.

Suddenly, the Governor's coffee kicked in and he was starting to get mountain mad. "If you're just gonna roll the roulette wheel and pick a suspect, why Campbell? That boy worked two jobs and helped put himself through college. He teaches Sunday School and takes elderly widow women to get their groceries."

"Someone on staff—a gardener I think—said he saw them arguing late afternoon on the front grounds. I can't attest to that, though. I was more involved with how I was going to satisfy the Houghtons than getting the name right. After I got off the phone, though, I got worried. Houghton told me that, at first, they thought it was an accident. Then, upon further investigation, decided it was murder. Cage, here's another problem—and this needs to be just between us—I'm afraid this young man is being railroaded. Just like you said. They need someone to pin the murder on, *IF* it was even murder. My conscience won't let me stand by for that to happen."

Cager tried to hold his voice steady. "Mississippi is a fine state. One of my favorite places to visit but, dadgum, I won't have a young man's life ruined to save the reputation of a family which, it sounds, has already done a lot of reputation ruining on their own. I absolutely need to get involved. Tell me this, am I supposed to make up a murder if it were, in fact, a drunken fall, down the stairs?"

"McCager Burnett you know me better than that. Be honest. Just be sure you get it right."

CR

Chatty looked at the large Kubota truck and the extended cab truck that seated four, comfortably. He summed it up in his mind: if he went in the Kubota, he'd get dusty and dirty. He had already seen how the sand-covered road clouded up when another vehicle took off. But the truck smelled of grease, sweat, and the seats were covered in dirt. Too, he must be careful how he chose because Stella would lecture him.

Hmmmm.

"Stella, what are you riding in?" he asked, trying to keep his voice steady.

"The Kubota. They're always so much fun. We had a similar, small one made by John Deere, on the farm. My sister, Lynn, and I had so many laughs while flying around in it. The way we drove, it's a wonder that nobody ever got killed."

Pepper piped up, "Let me guess. You want to ride with Stella."

"Pepper!" Chatty exclaimed. "What a brilliant idea!"

The Governor tried to hide his smile. He knew that Chatty's pristine outfit, which looked like something Rosalind Russell might've worn in *Auntie Mame*, would make him look like a field hand by the time the ride to the Big House was over—but he just couldn't resist the idea.

"Pepper," the Governor said. "Really, you should ride with me and Sanders. Not only is he a DNR officer who lives on this island and knows every particle of sand, he can tell us about the alleged murder." McCager then turned to Sanders, "I presume that the Sheriff will meet us at the house?"

"Yes, sir. He spent the night on the island. He's eager to see you."

Chatty hopped into the Kubota while the Governor climbed in the truck. Cager could not suppress a laugh as the open-doored Kubota took off, rather roughly, and nearly threw Chatty out.

Chatty turned, sheer terror on his face, to look at Stella, in the back seat, and it was obvious how petrified he was.

But it was nothing compared to how dusty his equestrian outfit would be after only a few minutes. It was not a happy day for Chatty.

ભ

The Reynolds Mansion was surrounded by yellow crime tape. The picturesque fountain in the front of the house was shut off so that it didn't spray water in the air. Stella and Pepper, both, were stunned to see such a grand house on an island even though it was over sixteen thousand acres, with another four or five hundred acres being recognized at Gullah Geechee land. On the way from the ferry to the house, the open-air Kubota, leading the truck, would slow or stop completely when Stella wanted to see something.

"Oh, look!" Stella remarked, pointing to St. Luke's Baptist Church, with three peaks and a steeple with a bell and a cross. It had an inside porch, three steps with a railing, a wheelchair ramp, and green-painted shutters. Stella asked the driver to stop.

The Governor and Pepper stepped out of the truck. "Pepper, do you know what that table is for? The one setting outside, under those wonderful, big trees?"

He shook his head then commented, "What a sweet church. I can hear them singing "Amazing Grace." No, why the table?"

"Does anyone care that I am covered completely in white dirt?" Chatty asked.

"No," replied Stella and Pepper in unison.

"We are more concerned with the table," Pepper replied, slapping Chatty on the shoulder in a friendly gesture. Chatty lifted his large girth out of the Kubota and began dusting himself off.

Stella smiled. "At Mt. Pisgah, the little church where I grew up at Turner's Corner, every fourth Sunday of July, we had homecoming. It was a big day. People who'd lived there but had moved away, came back and joined with those still there, to celebrate. Our church women made the most delicious food and covered the table—ours was cement on blocks—with tablecloths and food. Every woman had her specialty. Mama's was fresh-made chicken and dumplings and Mrs. Cora Nix was known for her cakes and pies. No one brought just one dish. They loaded their cars down so we'd have plenty of food."

Chatty, of course, glanced up from preening himself. *"You ate outside among the bugs and the buzzards?"* He shuddered and more dust fell from his fancy jacket. "Please. Please. *Please.* Don't tell me that you ate from *paper plates and drank from Dixie cups."*

"No," Stella replied.

"Thank the Lord." Chatty looked upward and raised his hands in praise.

"We drank from red, Solo cups. They're plastic."

The Governor was climbing back into the truck. "Hey, Stella, we need to be going. We have a lot to do, and I feel quite sure the Sheriff will want to get home for supper." He grinned. "I've eaten Miss Eula Mae's cooking and I can promise we wouldn't want to miss it, either. Best cornbread I ever had in my life."

"I think I'll ride in the Kubota the rest of the way," Pepper said.

Chatty heaved. "Oh, boy," he mumbled. As Chatty strained, trying to lift himself into the back seat, Pepper gallantly suggested, "You sit up front with Stella. She can squeeze in between you and the driver"—which Stella did but a portion of Chatty still hung outside the Kubota as they bumped along the road. The driver pointed out the lovely white house where the DNR director lived. In the yard was a swing set for his kids. An old, yellow lab looked up from his nap and watched as the two vehicles passed. Then, he went back to sleep. Life on Sapelo, surrounded by water and quiet, seemed perfect. It was all so simple and sweet.

Then they reached the Reynolds House and were taken aback by its incredible grandeur. It was a stunning sight.

Stella's mouth dropped open, Pepper's eyes widened, and Chatty clapped his hands together in delight, like a small child, and exclaimed, "Now, *these* are *my* people!"

Except for Cager and the DNR folks who already knew its beauty, the Big House was wonderful to behold—a remarkable Federalist House that set like a crown jewel in the midst of the landscape, surrounded by enormous live oaks that wept with moss. Though he knew its beauty well, for a moment, McCager Burnett felt ashamed that he had gotten so used to such a gorgeous setting that his heart no longer skipped when he saw it, like it used to, once upon long ago.

"How did a place like this get all the way over to the island?" Stella asked in an awestruck voice.

"By boat," the Governor replied. "Piece by piece." He chuckled. The Governor was a big country music fan and could quote lyrics to most songs, especially older ones. "Like the old Johnny Cash lyrics written by Wayne Kemp—'They got it here one piece at a time. But it did cost more than a dime'."

"R.J. Reynolds, Jr. built this?" asked Pepper while Chatty wandered around the lush yard, beneath the hanging moss, like a starstruck child lost in a magic kingdom.

The Governor shook his head. "No, it started with a plantation farmer in the late 1700s, named Spalding. He was a genius. He developed what's known as Sea Island Cotton. It's a long, very fine and soft cotton strand."

Deputies and Georgia Bureau of Investigation officers surrounded the house while the quartet walked about. "When Howard Coffin bought the island, the house was falling apart. He cleaned it up, added on, put fountains in, then added landscaping. Richard, as R.J. Jr. was known, added an inside pool and upstairs room that's known as the circus room."

"Do you think," Chatty asked in childlike wonderment, "That there's any old sterling silver inside?" Then, he stopped for a moment as a thrilling thought hit his mind. "Oh, my goodness. What if there is railroad silver in there?" He placed his right hand across his dusty jacket. "If there is, be still my heart." He closed his eyes and swayed in the dream he was having. "If there is railroad silver inside, I won't be able to take it. Have paramedics standing by."

Stella's face crumbled in puzzlement. "Railroad silver?"

Chatty, for certain, was about to have a heart attack now. He clutched at his suede, sand-covered vest. "Child, dear, beautiful, wonderful child. I beg your forgiveness for not teaching you better. I have failed you."

She frowned. "Stop with the theatrics."

Pepper, proud as punch, stepped forward. "I know all about railroad silver."

Chatty, "all a'sudden", came out of his dying stage, straightened up and looked at Pepper with a sour expression. He did not like for people to know more than he did about fabulous possessions of the wealthy. Especially a government employee. Working for a pension, nonetheless.

"And you know this how?" Chatty asked with a real attitude.

"My Aunt Dora Jennings inherited the collection of my great-Aunt Maude who'd been collecting railroad silver ever since '39 when she rode the Super Chief. She'd inherited coal mining money from her grandfather and was traveling by rail, from Chicago to Los Angeles, when she saw the movie star, Betty Grable, pouring coffee from a silver pot. She offered the steward a great deal of money to sell her the pot and he got permission and sold it to her."

"You haven't answered the question," Chatty replied, tartly. "What is railroad silver?"

"Each railroad had its own specially-designed silver service for first class. Stamped on the bottom of each piece is the railroad name—Santa Fe, Union, so on and so forth."

Chatty's face fell, miserably. Pepper was exactly right. He had been outdone by an up-and-comer. A public servant, no less.

Stella smiled from ear to ear. In all the time she'd known and loved Chatty, this was the first time she had ever seen him one-upped.

Chatty crossed his arms, thought for a second, then asked, "Who are the Harvey girls?"

"The Harvey—" and before Pepper could finish, Cager whistled.

"We're burnin' daylight. Let's get in here and start looking around."

With his hands in his pockets, Chatty dragged along, trailing behind Stella and Pepper, unaware of anything until a broad, heavily muscled arm slammed across his chest. "I'm sorry, sir. I don't have permission to allow you in." He was wearing a Georgia Bureau of Investigation vest.

The Governor was already up the steps, ready to enter the front door, when he turned and saw the startled look on Chatty's face which had a streak of muddy dirt running across his cheek.

"Aw, let him in," the Governor commanded. "He's just here to see the silver."

Chapter Ten

CR

Sheriff Goudelock met the group at the door and was introduced by the Governor, whom he had known since Goudelock was a young agent with the Georgia Bureau of Investigation, when he had worked several details with McCager Burnett.

Both men had a great deal of respect for the other. In fact, Governor Burnett had been so impressed with the young Goudelock that he recommended him for promotion. Twelve years ago, when the longtime Sheriff of McIntosh decided to retire at the age of 70 so "I can do some fishing 'fore I get to be an old-timer," the Governor called Goudelock and urged him to run for the position.

"It's your home county and no one has worked more traffic accidents, white collar crime, and a few murders here and there, than you have. This is the time that the Lord has prepared you for—to see after the welfare of the fine people of McIntosh County. You can take your state retirement, completely vested, then have fourteen or fifteen years as Sheriff."

If it had been up to him, Goudelock would have left Atlanta the next day and gone down to the courthouse and signed up. But, his wife, Eula Mae, took some convincing. She'd spent 30 years worrying every time he walked out the door that she might never see him again. Now, he had earned his retirement and, in her opinion, she had earned a rest, too.

Finally, their eldest son, LeRoy, a court bailiff, convinced his Mama that it wasn't a dangerous job (no one could remember a murder) but there were traffic accidents over on I-95 that passed through McIntosh and the meanest anyone in the county ever got was when Winnona Motes took off after her drunk husband with a frying pan. Once, she'd hit him with the backside of it before it had cooled down from frying bacon so, between the iron, the heat, and the scorching bacon grease, he never came home drunk again.

When Goudelock heard that story, he laughed and recalled the time he asked his grandfather what were the most important lessons he had learned in life.

His grandfather, with skin almost the color of a cast iron skillet and as weathered because of the years he spent working in the sun for the Department of Transportation, rocked back and forth and said, "Son, three things to always remember: Find the Lord before you need Him. That's first and foremost. Second, sad to say this, friends come and go but enemies accumulate. And, lastly, never fry bacon without a shirt on."

With Eula Mae convinced, Goudelock ran for office and had served quite happily for several years. This wasn't his first murder—but it was his first as Sheriff.

"Well, Governor, I never thought I'd ever see anything like this when I let you talk me into the Sheriff business. Not here on Sapelo."

Cager slapped him on the back and said, "But no finer man has ever been up to the task. Now, tell me, y'all thought it was an accident at first was what I heard. Our longtime housekeeper, Mrs. Puckett, had been wailing and a'cryin' something awful because her fine, young nephew had been arrested for murder. Then, come to find out, it's my good friend Jerome Goudelock who arrested him. How'd it turn from an accident so quickly?"

"Governor, you remember when I was a young GBI agent and I thought I knowed all there was to know?"

McCager nodded. "Yep. Remember it well. Seems like to me I recall Roscoe Bruner taking you to task once and straightening some of that know-it-all out of you."

"Yessiree. I needed it, too. Served me well. So, what goes 'round, comes 'round. We got a young Emory intern over in the coroner's office. We were all set to put this to bed as a drunk opening the door to a set of stairs. But he's convinced us to keep the case open. Trust me, I wanted it to be an accident and that's how I intended to write it up."

"What makes this young man think it's a murder?" asked Pepper.

"There's a wide smack across the victim's forehead. His neck is broken, which is what 'kilt' him, as my uncle says, but according to this young medical student, Joseph Maycomb, if he had stumbled accidentally, he would have been in a crouched position as he stumbled down the stairs. That beam is just under six feet high so he would have had to be propelled from a standing position, straight through the air, then hit the beam."

"That makes sense. And that would kill him, right there," Stella commented.

"Excuse my manners," apologized the Governor. "Let me make some introductions."

That done, the Sheriff said, "Miss Stella, that's the problem with law enforcement and murder. It isn't always like it looks. Oh, how I wish it were that easy. We have a wonderful medical examiner. But Joseph made a valid point. Come with me."

The group walked directly into the living room, still furnished with the expensive furniture that Richard Reynolds was using when he died in 1964. Two antique chandeliers hung from a solid wood-beamed ceiling. Stella, once, while on a trip with Asher, had driven up the coast of California and visited San Simeon, the famous William Randolph Hearst estate. The ceilings reminded her of Hearst's mansion. There were two beige, matching love seats facing each other and a heavy, antique, carved mahogany table. The stone fireplace, also carved, was impressive and above it hung a large, painted portrait of a stately man in a double-breasted Navy officer's jacket and a white yachting cap.

Stella stopped to look at the portrait. "Is that Mr. Reynolds?"

"Sure is," the Governor replied. "He loved sailing. Probably what attracted him to Sapelo—beautiful land surrounded by gorgeous blue water and alluring beach. I'll show you all that loveliness while we're here. He had a yacht. Even served with Naval intelligence during World War II. There was no one quite like him. Maybe Hemingway but I can't think of anyone else. He could drive or fly anything you put him in as well as captain a ship." McCager Burnett looked thoughtful for a moment, then his expression turned to sadness. "He died from emphysema." He shook his head, glancing around the room. "The very thing that gave him all this and so much more is what killed him at a fairly young age. As I get older, I see the irony in things such as that. He suffered terribly for a few years before dying. Well, talking about death, let's go take a look."

The living room led straight into a 1950's version of a commercial kitchen. Stella, full of the wonder that she was, looked all over the kitchen, lagging behind. Sheriff Goudelock opened a door, flipped on the light, then stepped out of the way for the group—except for Chatty who was already digging through the kitchen cabinets for the silver—who peered down a flight of steep stairs. At the bottom of the stairs was the chalk outline of a fairly large body.

"Follow me," said Sheriff Goudelock as he led the group down the steep staircase. Upon reaching the second to the last step, the 6'1" tall Sheriff turned and cautioned the others, "Watch your step."

There was no need for Stella to stoop but both Cager and Pepper dropped their heads, then stepped over the chalked outline.

"Where does this tunnel go?" asked Pepper.

"It was an underground passage for servants to move back and forth, across the house, without being seen."

The Sheriff then pointed to the outline. "He was lying, doubled up. The smell of whiskey was so strong it nearly knocked us over when we got here." Goudelock shook his head. "In fact, it was so bad that we're willing to say that it was Jack Daniel's Black. There's a unique smell to that whiskey."

Stella looked over at Pepper, remembering the night before when he had ordered it. Pepper started sniffing around, smelling the air, then bent down to smell the wood step and a hooked rug next to it. A smile slid sideways up his face.

"Sheriff, are you a drinker?"

"Oh, no. I'm a Baptist. My deputy is a Methodist. So is the medical examiner. They're the ones that told me."

"Well, they're good Methodists. They know what liquor they're talkin 'about. It's Jack Daniel's Black."

About that time, they all heard the familiar sound of Chatty calling out. "Helloooo! Where are my friends?"

They glanced up to see Chatty appear in the door.

"Oh, there y'all are. Y'all need to come see this incredible silver I found." He grabbed hold of the railing and started down the steps, but a terrible thing happened right before their eyes. Chatty missed the first step and started tumbling down, toward them.

It was a nightmare that took their breath away as they watched their beloved Chatty falling toward them.

Chapter Eleven

ℭℛ

Spencer Marcus Houghton was to the manor born. The Houghtons were to America what the Royals were to the British. Since the late nineteenthth century, every generation had increased the wealth of the previous generation. They had style, plenty of clout, and some looks. Mostly, they were a plain-looking bunch who decorated themselves up with such fashion and jewels that no one seemed to notice that their eyes were wide set and their noses were enormous.

They were all tall, including the women who often hovered near six feet, and had large hands. Of course, with that kind of wealth, the men were all able to marry beautiful women, but their unattractive bloodline always seemed to cancel out the beauty and, therefore, the children produced were normally plain. There was an exception. Eliza Houghton, Spencer's Aunt, seemed to spring out of nowhere with her dark, glistening locks, large blue eyes, and perfect smile. It was said, and said often, that Louis B. Mayer, the head of MGM studios, had tried to sign her to a movie contract. When she saw the amount he was offering (a fortune to most

Americans) she tossed back her lovely head and laughed merrily.

"Why, I spend more than that in a year on lipstick!"

But one thing Hollywood did bring Eliza was a husband. Roy Lively was movie star handsome which is why Fox Studio signed him in the first place. The problem? He couldn't act. So, when his contract was up, it wasn't renewed, leaving him to kick around town and make his rent by working as an extra. He made it a habit of having a drink every afternoon at the Chateau Marmont where all the wealthy people stayed. It was there that he met Eliza and fell instantly in love—without knowing how rich she was. The Houghtons' best chance at producing beauty was with these two but, alas, they were never able to bear children. This sad fact eventually drove Eliza to become a rich eccentric who usually had a dozen cats and several dogs sitting on sofas that were custom-made for $25,000. As for Roy, he took up drinking full-time and gambling part-time, living until a stroke took him out at seventy-eight while Eliza lived until eight-three. She left some of her fortune to charity but most of it to her favorite nephew—Spencer.

That put Spencer on the Forbes list of the 50 Wealthiest Americans. He also served on the company's board of directors, his father having appointed him after declaring he was the only child he had who had any sense. Spencer was twenty-four when he joined the board and discovered that he enjoyed the pharmaceutical business so much that he became the first

Houghton in three generations to actually work in the company.

"I'm a legalized drug dealer," he liked to joke. He was different from the rest of the family because he was down-to-earth and very likable. He was kind to everyone and always a gentleman to the ladies. He stood when one entered a room and always opened the door for others.

When Spencer started at the company, his first job was as receptionist. The woman who normally handled the job was severely ill so he worked that job for two weeks. Then, he went to the mailroom for two months which endeared him to all employees. Cheerfully, he delivered the mail every day and picked up whatever needed to be mailed out.

Spencer was a true example of the sort of people who come from the Mississippi Delta. It's a slower pace of life there and people are friendlier which might have been a mighty influence on his outlook on life.

Sales is where the real money was and, other than research and development, it is the lifeline for drug companies. So, Spencer wanted to learn that side of the company. The Vice President of the company suggested that he ride with their top salesman, Ance McCoy, for a month. He had met Ance briefly when he was working the reception desk. But riding in a car together, for hours at a time, caused them to develop a deep friendship.

Ance grew up in the Delta, too. His family was far from wealthy. In fact, they struggled every month to make ends meet. Ance knew the meaning of "hard living" and always recalled the times the family would subsist on soup beans and cornbread—often for a week or more. To add to the difficulty, Ance's mother was mean and rough with her kids. None of her four children could remember a kind word of praise that she had ever given them. She had once been a beauty but her bitterness for the sparse life she had to live had stolen her looks. The corners of her mouth were turned down and there was always a furrow between her eyes. The closest thing she ever came to a smile was when that furrow disappeared—for only a fleeting moment.

Ance's father worked the cotton fields for a local planter. He was a hard laborer, but his earning oftentimes fell short of seeing to all his family's needs, especially if there had been an emergency like the time Ance had to have his wisdom teeth removed. When he thought back on his childhood, Ance always grimaced at the constant arguing between his parents and all the times he was told, "We don't have the money for that."

At ten years old, Ance wanted a pair of sneakers like the other kids wore and, of course, there was no money to buy them. With a load of gumption, he called up the local newspaper and asked if there was a route available for him to deliver papers. The family lived in Greenville, Mississippi, which was home to one of the country's finest newspapers, *The Greenville Delta Democrat-Times*. It and its publisher were highly regarded and admired by newspaper people in every state. Hodding Carter II was the paper's publisher and he had been both a Neiman Fellow and a Pulitzer Prize winner for writing an editorial on the intolerance of Japanese Americans who had fought in World War II. He had built the newspaper into a formidable force. In fact, his power was so great that the Kennedys sought his friendship and support. Carter also became a footnote to history for having dinner with Bobby Kennedy, in Los Angeles, on the night before he was assassinated at the Ambassador Hotel. Carter learned of the assassination on the plane, returning home, then over-heard a man make an unkind remark about Kennedy. In his tremendous grief, Carter could not hold back, and he punched the man in the mouth. His son, Hodding Carter III, became famous in his own right as a member of President Jimmy Carter's staff and as a television commentator.

There wasn't a paper delivery route available, immedi-ately, but a man from the newspaper called about a month later and offered Ance a job. With all his might and enthusi-asm, he did his job well. In addition to delivering newspapers, if he could bring in new customers, he would receive a com-mission. This was when Ance learned that he had a true gift for selling. He quickly made enough money to buy the sneak-ers and, from then on, he never asked his parents for another dime. Once, his mother had snapped at him angrily, then dropped down into a kitchen chair and began to sob. Ance had never seen his mother cry. He stood affixed to the ground for a minute, watching the unusual sight, then inched over to her and gingerly put his hand on her shoulder.

"Uh, is everything okay?" he asked tentatively, afraid that she might turn around and hit him. She beat on her children quite regularly, but she only did it when their father wasn't around. They loved the weekends when he was home because they didn't have to be fearful of being hit. Mr. McCoy didn't allow it.

She shook her head and continued crying. Without a word, she handed Ance a piece of paper. It was a cut-off notice from the power company. The amount owed was $21.43. Ance had $27 saved up so he went to the room he shared with his brother and pulled out a cigar box, from under his bed. Removing $22 from the box, then wrapping the rubber band back around it, he walked to the kitchen.

"Here, Mama. This is money I saved."

She looked up from her crying and saw the one-dollar bills in his hand. For the only time in his life, his Mother reached out and awkwardly hugged him. That hug was worth a million dollars to Ance. When she died, it was the only kind memory of her that he could recall.

His father, who outlived her by several years, once said shortly before his death, "It was a hard life for all of us because of her. But, son, some people have pain that goes so far down that it can't ever be healed." He stared into space for a moment then, choosing his words carefully, he said, "It was a generational curse. She got it from her father who got it from his father. Best as I could gather, it went all the way back to her great-Grandfather. They were all mean people."

Spencer Houghton, on the other hand, had a completely different life. He grew up in a mansion filled with servants and new Cadillacs back in the day when a Cadillac meant real wealth. His mother, who was kind and gracious, spent much of her time with garden clubs and the Junior Service League. She volunteered for every committee at their Episcopal church. Her name was Grace and everyone said it suited her well. His father never worked a job, choosing to live off his dividends—"mailbox money" he called it. Mostly, he played golf or poker with his buddies and during the times he was home, he was reading.

"A well-read man is well-educated man," he liked to say.

Spencer, in a stable home, excelled at academics, football, and basketball. On the nights that he played a game, his family did not miss it. His parents and siblings were in the stands, cheering him on. He chose to go to Vanderbilt—far enough away from home but not too far—and there, he regularly made the Dean's List.

Once, his father had said to his mother, "Grace, why does that boy try so hard? He is never going to need more wealth than he will have." This, he said, even before he knew that Eliza would leave her wealth to Spencer.

"Dear," replied Grace, "not everyone is like you. Some want to enjoy the pure pleasure of making a career for themselves."

He eyed her warily, not exactly sure what she meant by that, so he just shrugged and went to the country club to play golf.

The difference between these two young men was monumental. Yet, they became the best of friends, closer than the closest brothers. Each served as best man at their first weddings. Then Spencer was witness to Ance's second wedding at the courthouse. When Spencer's wife just up and left him, Ance was there through it all. Since there were no children, it was a pretty easy divorce because she wanted out so badly. Still, Spencer was devastated and quite sure he would not have made it through without Ance's counseling and friendship. They climbed up the corporate ladder, side by side until, finally, Spencer became Chairman and CEO with Ance serving as his trusty CFO. They had been at those positions for close to eight years when they made that fateful voyage to Sapelo Island for a corporate retreat.

Neither could ever have predicted, nor believed, what would happen in the Reynolds House.

Chapter Twelve

CR

Governor McCager, Stella, and Pepper were wordlessly stunned and horrified as they watched Chatty fall, attired in his dusty equestrian outfit, dropping his little horse whip. He did not, however, let go of a small, sterling silver teapot he had discovered in one of the counters.

As he bumped, bumped down the stairs, Pepper, a quick-thinking US Marshal—though he had never faced a situation quite like this before—quickly moved to the first step and threw his body toward Chatty in effort to stop his thunderous descent. He came down the best way possible, feet first.

Chatty's size twelve boot smacked Pepper's face in one of the hardest hits he had ever felt. Well, there was the time a monster-size of guy slapped him, hand opened, when the Marshals had attempted to arrested him for racketeering in Chicago. That slap sent Pepper reeling backward and flipping over several chairs until he landed on his back, on top of a table. His buddy, Charlie Fair, ran over to check on Pepper after Charlie had punched the giant so hard that he crumpled to the ground. Charlie's punch had broken his jaw and knocked out two teeth. While he moaned and heaved, other

Marshals, completely without mercy, picked up the racketeer, read him his rights, and carried him out to a waiting car where they cuffed him and threw him inside.

Later, it was determined that Chatty was alright, though he had ripped the armhole on the left side of his suit only because he had refused to let go of the beautiful, ancient sterling silver teapot. Stella was the first to him, stroking his face and sweetly comforting her dear Chatty.

The Governor was less sympathetic. "Chatty, are you alright? Can you stand up?" He was sitting on the second step from the bottom. "I think I am. My neck isn't broken. Is it? I thank God for that. Running bingo every Thursday at the church has really blessed me." This time, when he repeated this oft-used phrase of his, it was humbly and without bragging.

"Oh, Chatham, you running a bingo game—a gambling game if you get right down to it—has nothing to do with God blessing you. Though, I'm quite sure He is grateful for your unique ministry. Here, let's help you stand up." The Governor had no time for such foolishness.

With the Governor on one side and tiny Stella on the other, they managed to get Chatty on his feet. Though he resisted, unusually, a bit in an attempt to elicit sympathy. Stella hoped that he was uninjured but was also well aware of how her friend could play out sickness for a long time. Not because he was selfish but because she realized that he was lonely and craved attention.

Chatty stretched his back and cracked his neck to make it pop. He turned to Stella and asked, "Is there a mark on my flawless face?" It was the dirt that McCager had spotted earlier.

That's when they realized that Chatham Balsam Colquitt IV was going to live, to strive another day to aggravate. They were much relieved.

"Chatham, you scared me to death!" Stella declare. "It was a terrible sight to see but thank goodness Pepper acted so quickly. "Oh goodness! We forgot about Pepper."

There, sitting on an upper step, rubbing his side and holding his head, Pepper said, sarcastically," Don't worry, I'm used to coming in second to Chatham, His Majesty."

Chatty, for his part, smiled happily. "Thank you for such a keen observation." He winked.

Sheriff Goudelock said, "If you don't mind, we need you to stay off the chalk outline." Chatty looked down and, rather horrified, jumped away. "*That's* where he was murdered?" Chatty took it all in and looked rather unnerved.

Stella was now tending to Pepper—in a loving manner which he happily noticed. He had a cut on his forehead, not enough to require stitches but he leaned over to Stella and whispered, "I think that I have a cracked rib."

"Oh, Pepper!"

"Listen, don't tell anyone, but I'll need a good taping-up tonight." He grinned. "And I might need you to do it for me." He sighed. "Though, I will have to shave the chest area where the tape goes." He smiled. "Will that bother you?"

She blushed a bit. "I've been married before. I've seen a bare chest. You think I'm more naïve than I am." She straightened up and pulled forth her full gumption—"umption" as her mountain people said "I realized I don't know everything but I do consider myself worldly." Then, dropping her eyes, she added, "Somewhat." He looked at her askance and she shifted from one foot to another.

"Well, kinda. I was on the racing circuit, remember? I learned a lot there! I saw Richard Petty get taped up in the garage, once, after a practice accident. He's one of the tougher men I ever met.

He said, 'Don't take me to that diddly wink of a hospital. Just tape me up here."

Stella giggled. "He got a sponsor from Goody's crushed aspirin. Oh, I wish I had a dime for every time he walked through the garage throwing back a pack of that Goody's powder and swallowing it without a single drop of water. Gosh, I loved him and truly admire him. Back to the subject."

Pepper let it go because she did get off the subject a good bit. "Proceed, my fair lady."

"I think you think I'm less sophisticated than I am."

"You've barely scratched the surface," he laughed.

Meanwhile, Chatty was growing restless. "Excuse me." He pointed to himself. "I was the one who was hurt. I hurtled down from the top of the stairs. I might need surgery or, God forbid, never walk again.

"You're walking fine now," Pepper retorted, realizing that he was picking up the same tone that Stella used with their darling Chatty.

Sheriff Goudelock, who had been in a deep conversation with McCager, spoke. "Mr. Colquitt, one of our medical professionals is just across the waterway from the island. I've radioed him and he'll be on his way. Now, let me warn you of one little thing—he's our intern from Emory. He's eager. And he's smart. But by the time he's finished with you, he may find all kinds of things wrong." He turned his back so Chatty wouldn't see his grin.

Chatty's blue eyes widened. "What kinds of things? Oh, I'm not ready for this. Sheriff, I'm not ready to go to heaven." Here, he lifted an eye and looked quite serious. "As glorious as heaven seems to be, I worry that it's a long drop down from my quality of life, here, on earth." Chatty straightened up and patted his knees. "No, I'm quite happy here. I don't need to die. Tell your medical person that I'm perfectly okay."

Chatty held out the piece of silver that he had clung to tenaciously as he stumbled toward potential death. It was a sterling silver gravy boat, handcrafted around 1880. Chatty had spent a goodly portion of his time, studying silver. "For instance, look at this exquisite masterpiece. Sterling silver is easily dented which is why I protected it at the risk of my life." He paused and put his hand on his hip which wasn't bruised and asked, "Did you ever dream that there was such grandeur?" He held it gingerly, treasuring it like a baby with a new teddy bear.

Sheriff Goudelock, a deacon who knew the Bible frontward and backwards yet who had just seen the real Chatham, didn't know whether to laugh or to be stunned. "I have never heard anyone refer to the glory of heaven as being a letdown or disappointment."

Cager laughed and said, "Welcome to our world!"

The Sheriff then said," We don't see much like Mr. Colquitt down here in McIntosh County. We is poor people down this way. I don't think there is a millionaire amongst us." Though educated, the Sheriff held onto the language he'd grown up hearing. He found that it served him well with many of the people in the county, most especially on Sapelo and with the Gullah Geechees. He worked hard on not acting high falutin'.

"Mr. Colquitt, you may have done been very important in solvin' this mystery" the Sheriff said but did not elaborate.

"Maybe you're a hero again!" cheered Stella.

Chatty grinned from ear-to-ear. Apparently, he had saved the day once more. In his mind, he thought yet did not say it, *It would be a sad, sad world without me.*

He was happy beyond words.

Chapter Thirteen

ભ

While the others chattered amongst themselves, Sheriff
Goudelock made a call to the Darien Medical Examiner's office and had them patch him through to Theodore at home.

"Hey, Theodore, did I wake you? I'm sorry. When can
you send Joseph over on a special boat I'll be requesting?"
Goudelock glanced at his watch. "It's 11:30. We got the boat
and captain ready to go. Have 'im bring all his files and anything he needs with him. You stay there over yonder for some
shut eye. We'll send for you if we ain't gettin' this wrapped
up fast enough."

Then, the Sheriff listened for a couple of minutes to Mr.
Rascal. "No, ain't nothin' wrong but we accidentally—and,
boy if that ain't the word for it—gave a good test to his theory
of Houghton knockin' his head in a push rather than a tum-
ble. No, not at all, you're the best I've seen in Georgia. You're
not in trouble. Just send him over quick as possible. I want
him to fully work out his theory. Call someone else in your
office to stay there so you can get some sleep. We ain't as
young as we were this time last year. Them days done gone.
Come if you want but you've earned a rest. Make up for it.
Thanks. Bye."

Meanwhile, Chatty was dancing around and wiggling his bottom which wiggled quite liberally. "I've done again! Saved the day." He sighed, "Who would have ever thought that I—the little boy that Asher and his buddies tormented with such unkindness—would turn out to be a master crime solver. And Asher's in prison. Federal prisoner, no less!!" He squeezed his hands together. "The Lord is so good. I'm telling you—it's the bingo."

McCager gave him one of his "calm down" looks that he would have given to one of his legislators. "Calm down, Mr. Too-Big-For-Your-Britches-Much-Too-Soon. Nothing is solved yet. We have what is called a 'theory.'"

Chatty stopped dancing. He looked crestfallen.

"To begin with, Chatty, you don't know what we know at this point. Or think. Although all is a hypothesis now."

"But it's possible?" Chatty asked, hopeful.

Chatty sighed and smiled. "I believe. I believe that all those nights I helped out with senior bingo will come back to reward me."

The Governor, clearly perplexed, said, "I don't think that 'reward' is the word I would use. After all, we are not at the country club, playing golf, and aiming for trophies."

"Oh, did you hear?" Chatty asked, suddenly changing the subject. "I gave up golf. I told everyone it was because of a bad knee but it was really all the sweat and what it did to my hair. Talk about a mess. I needed an excuse to sound legitimate." He paused and looked pensive. "Besides, they worship gossip more than women or the beauty shop and I just can't tolerate such unseemliness." He smiled like an angel who had just earned his wings. As though he knew what the others were thinking, he said gaily, "Just like Clarence in *It's A Wonderful Life*. You know, I still cry every time that ZuZu or whatever her name is, says, 'Listen, Daddy. A bell is ringing. Teacher says that every time a bell rings, an angel gets its wings'." Chatty teared up, pulled his monogrammed handkerchief from his pocket, and wiped at his eyes.

All three stared at him in disbelief.

"Do you live in a fairytale where you are the star *all* the time?" asked the Governor because no one else could say it and get away with it.

"Well, if you're talking about my beautiful houses and servants and possessions, yes, I do." But something occurred to him. "But you're not talking about something other than what I could possibly comprehend, are you?"

The Governor rolled his eyes and shook his head. "Yes, Chatty, I'm talking about something you could never understand."

"Well, to make you feel better, Governor, and you do seem distressed, I'm thinking of going back to golf, just for nine holes. And the gossip, of course. But if I find out that they're saving the best gossip until the last nine holes, I'll go back to the complete eighteen." No one ever believed Chatty was leaving any tidbit of gossip on a golf course—or anywhere else.

McCager Burnett turned mountain red with anger. If one has never seen it, one should take this advice: avoid it at all costs. Stella, quite an expert on such, changed the subject quickly.

"Hey, Chatty," Stella said cheerfully as she pulled her hair back into a band, then situated the hat on top of her head for a day out—plus it was chilly in the basement and her jacket was in the Kubota, "Why don't you go outside and play? Not golf, of course." She laughed a little, knowing there wasn't a golf course on Sapelo and, most likely, never would be because the state controlled it. So, even if another millionaire like Howard Coffin or Richard Reynolds came along, even they could not put a golf course on Sapelo Island.

"Play—what?" he asked, quizzically. Then, after momentarily looking skeptical, as if he were being brushed off, he realized what Stella meant.

"My precious, green-eyed Stella, you are right!" While Stella escorted Chatty up the stairs, he excitedly prattled, saying, "I do want to look at the wonderful terraces where romances came into being and orchestras played. I wonder if Harry James ever played here with his big band and pleased the dinner audiences. Which reminds me, when will we be eating? I don't want to be late. That would be immeasurably rude of me." Chatty's voice drifted off as McCager and Pepper shared a look of relief, with McCager sitting down, joining Pepper on the steps. After a moment of quiet, Pepper offered, "Even down here, in the basement, you can almost hear the parties going on, upstairs."

"Oh yes, there was a lot of party going on here. Richard Reynolds was not a man who shied away from the enormous pleasures of life. He shared his good fortune with everyone—though I don't think the Gullah Geechees were ever invited to the parties. Still, he was very good to them and treated them well. He had everything." McCager stopped for a moment then added, "Everything except maybe for God. I never got the impression that religion was important to Richard Reynolds. The way I've seen it happen so many times, a man has all kinds of happiness, but he misses the joy. And, most important, he misses what comes after the party's over here on this earth."

McCager turned to Pepper who stayed quiet with his eyes downcast. He was hard to read. Perhaps that was something Pepper had learned as a law enforcement officer, McCager wondered. Maybe it was why he was so good at his job.

And then, before McCager could say anything more, the Sheriff returned, asking, "Should we get on down to business?"

Immediately, Pepper stood, jumping into it. "My first question is where are all the suspects? Wasn't this a corporate retreat?" Pepper walked over to some broken shards of glass still laying on the floor. "Was it determined that Houghton was holding a glass at the time of his fall? Or his push?"

"He was," the Sheriff noted," An expensive crystal glass."

"Of Jack Daniel's Black?" Pepper asked, wanting more clarity.

"Seems so," Goudelock shrugged. Then, continuing, "It soaked his shirt. We'll have a sample pretty quick." He chuckled, "There's a forensic expert in Brunswick who said the same as you: smelled like Jack Daniel's Black. Nevertheless, we're checking officially."

While crouching down and getting a closer look at the glass, Pepper opined, softly and slowly," I'm not married. Never have been and I don't have children." Just then, Pepper noticed Stella had returned, standing on the stairs, and suddenly he felt somewhat self-conscious—though he didn't exactly know why. He always felt that folks who work closely together should know about each other. Once, he knew a Marshal in Knoxville who refused to talk about himself. Maybe it was a coincidence, but that guy never got promoted. Years later, he retired only two minor ranks higher than when he started.

Stella smiled at Pepper and he smiled back—and the Governor could see how she had a fancy for him and he for her. Then Pepper said, "I guess why I didn't get married is women always want children... then the children need braces and tutoring and college... I'm a pragmatic, West Tennessee fellow," Pepper winked teasingly at Stella. He was feeling comfortable again, having retreated behind his sense of humor. None of this, of course, had escaped Stella's observation of Pepper. And she paid close attention. Once, she'd failed to pay that kind of attention to a man's character and she wound up marrying him. But never again.

"I wonder why this evidence wasn't collected until today," Pepper commented, indicating the broken glass.

"'Cause by the time I knowed yu'uns was a-comin', I guarded the place and waited for the GBI. We don't have that kind of skilled manpower in this county."

"That makes good sense," McCager said.

"I agree," concurred Pepper, "and I'd best not contaminate the crime scene should the GBI want to take a second look." Pepper stood up then, giving a quick wink to Stella, he passed her and headed up the stairs. He wasn't so comfortable as he thought.

Pepper had joked about marriage and children to avoid any discussion of it. The truth of the matter is that Pepper had an aunt with Cerebral Palsy who lived with his mother. His father had been dead several years, and Mrs. Culpepper felt it was her duty, because small town West Tennessee people were just this way, that a widow should take care of her husband's sister. Too, she loved Violet though, at seventy-four, Violet wore Pepper's mother down to the bone who, herself, was seventy-two and refused to send Violet to a nursing home. She took Violet to therapy twice a week to work with the sweetest and prettiest tall, blonde therapist with a cheerful attitude and loads of compassion. Someone told Anne Culpepper that Nicole McMillian had been a beauty queen and honor graduate before marrying a law student, putting him through school, then having five children, including a set of identical twins.

One day, Anne was watching Nicole as she finished up with an elderly patient. Nicole held her hands, then smiled brightly while looking the woman in the eyes. That was one thing that Anne had noticed—people often looked away from the disabled and elderly.

"Now, listen to me," Nicole was saying. "We're going to make you better. We're going to fix your back. You'll need to work with me and do everything I say. And if you do, we'll have you doing jumping jacks!" Nicole smiled from ear-to-ear. And the woman? She was beaming and nodding. "I promise, whatever you tell me to do, I will." With a withered hand, she reached up, touching Nicole's cheek and said, "Thank you. Most don't care about an old, nothin' like me."

Nicole reached over and hugged her. "I tell you—let's go to the Lord in prayer and ask Him in helping me to heal you."

Right there, in a therapy room, they prayed a short but meaningful prayer. By the next time, someone else asked to pray. By the third week, it was routine for them all to hold hands and pray, together. Once, when Pepper was there, having taken his Aunt Violet for his mother who'd had a migraine, he was astounded when one of the old men asked him, "You ain't gonna pray with us, son? I heard that Jesus appreciates at least one prayer ever so often." Pepper smiled and said, "Why, I sure am." And, from that day forward, they started each therapy session in the Lord's Prayer, this happening after circling the room with a request from each person.

"Nicole, I think you may be the whole reason we're here and Violet is in that chair. The Lord needed a link to a lot of people," Anne Culpepper remarked one day.

She threw back her head of perfectly-curled hair and said, "Well, I get a lot of practice by praying for my children Jon, Nix, Zoe, Aslyn and Bree. For playing sports and many other things, they need a lot of prayer! Besides, I believe in it, mightily."

Pepper put aside a bit for savings and pension (the same pension that Chatty laughed at which Pepper was unaware of, for had he known, his heart would have been crushed) and spent the rest of his salary—after living expenses, on his Mama and Aunt. One reason he had taken the Glynco training job several years ago, was that it gave him a free place to live and a stipend to eat on. He usually spent three months at Glynco, sometimes six, then went back into the field. He liked it and it kept his skills sharp so he could be a better training officer.

No one—not even Stella knew. And that's the way he wanted it.

Chapter Fourteen

❧

Joseph, with more than his usual enthusiasm, was headed for the island to set about proving the theory that he had developed. Plus, he had received a call that his grandfather had taken a turn for the better which greatly improved his spirits.

"Now, Joseph," warned his grandmama who everyone call Big Bessie—for obvious reasons and because she put up with no foolishness—"Don't git up them high hopes of yu'un. Old Solomon is a sick man. Even the biblical Solomon died. People 'round here say, 'You gotta get better before you die." She half-chuckled, "I used to sit with this woman who always had sumptin' wrong with her. Good for me because I's sittin' up with her to save money for your mama to marry that worthless daddy of you'un." She laughed again. "Aw, I'm just kiddin'. Fine man. Works hard. Not a lot of 'em around these parts work like Hank Maycomb. Anytime she got partway sick, she'd lift up off her death bed and say weakly, 'Is it time for me to cross right yet?'"

"I'd assure her it weren't near time because she was too mean. The next morning, she'd be up, bright-eyed and bushy-tailed, as we like to say. I'm tellin' you son, again, don't get yu'un's hopes high. We don't know what the Lord has in store."

But in his heart, Joseph believed it was going to be a great day. His Grandpappy wasn't ready for his time to come, and Joseph was out to solve his first murder on beautiful Sapelo Island.

The ferry delivered Joseph and all his paraphernalia at the wharf. The last ferry had already run for the day but, truth be told, Joseph felt special having the ferry all to himself. Sanders, from the DNR, was there to pick him up in an extended cab truck. Joseph, though, noticed that someone climbed out of the passenger's side and waited on Joseph before climbing in the back. In Sparta, they were always suspicious of people they didn't know. They stuck mostly to their own people because they knew their odd ways.

"You must be the brilliant young med student I've heard all about." This softened Joseph's heart a great deal. "I'm US Marshal Jackson Culpepper. You know how it is in the South. Your Mama's last name is the first child's first name." He grinned. "Most people call me Pepper. I'd be honored to have you call me that."

Pepper offered his hand and the handshake proved that the two men were destined to be strong friends and stronger allies. "Joseph Maycomb. I come from a little place call Sparta."

"Oh, I know Sparta. I arrested three or four here and there in Hancock County. One was a woman who was kiting checks. Remember that one well because she nearly broke my shinbone with the toughest kick I've ever felt."

"That must have been Sophie Alma Titley. Meanest woman in Sparta."

Sanders was waiting for others to move out of the way before putting the truck in gear and driving through the small crowd waiting to board the ferry. Joseph stared at the beautiful place, the marsh, the hanging moss, the smell of sea salt mixed together. He believed it to be the prettiest place he had ever seen. Nature pretty. Not man-made pretty. He said nothing more because he didn't want the men to know how small his world was—but also because he wanted to enjoy every second of it. The night of the murder he saw very little and was otherwise distracted by the victim's demise.

Pepper leaned forward, placing his hands between Sanders and Joseph in the front seat. "Before we get to the Reynolds House, let's talk about what you know."

Joseph explained that it didn't seem right, though perhaps it was possible, for a man Houghton's size to fall down the stairs in the tumbling position, head over heels, and have a high cement board hit his forehead so hard that it left a terrible mark.

No one disagreed that Houghton's neck had been broken in the fall and that it was possibly the cause of death—but people have survived a broken neck.

"If I'm correct, it could have been a terrible brain injury that did as much, or worse, than a broken neck or a broken back. The way I see it: if he had been pushed hard from the top of the stairs, as tall as he is, he would have traveled down eleven steps, airborne, and hit that beam, killing him. A traumatic head injury, broken neck, broken back—he died from at least two of those injuries. And it was not a mere drunken stumble.

"When'll the autopsy results be available?" Pepper asked.

"If it was you or me? Three to five months. A bigwig like Houghton, whose family has so much money? No more than two weeks. They're on order from Georgia, following a call from Mississippi where the Houghtons live, to get it done. It might even be next week."

Pepper nodded, sitting back wordlessly, staring out the window of the truck as they passed a few houses painted in bright blue, orange, yellow and any other colors. Not another word was said until the truck pulled up to the Reynolds House where, again, Joseph stared. He still couldn't get over such a wonderful mansion. He was speechless.

The three men then jumped out of the truck, and, within seconds, Stella came down the steps in a pretty orange, bell-sleeved dress with orange Kate Spade covered-toe flats.

She waved cheerfully and walked over. "You must be Joseph. My name's Stella Bankwell."

"Pleased to meet you, Ma'am."

About that time, the foursome heard a screeching like nothing they'd ever heard. It was frightening. Turning to the heavily wooded area from where the noise came, within seconds, they now heard a man screaming, "Help me! Help me! Please, a wild beast is chasing me!"

They thought they recognized the voice—though it was two octaves higher than usual. And before they could process what was happening, they looked to see Chatty, running as hard as anyone had ever seen—as matter of fact, no one had ever seen—Chatty run. He moved so fast that his knees high-stepped to his waist.

Stella looked over to see Pepper unsnap his holster and Sanders reached into the back seat to retrieve his rifle.

"What could it be?" Pepper asked Sanders.

But before Sanders could answer, Chatty emerged from the woods, into a clearing, the "wild beast" right on his heels.

"A cow?" Pepper asked, incredulously. Lowering his gun, Pepper turned to Sanders, "You have cows on this island? How in the world —?"

Sanders watched the cow, enjoying the sight. "I'll explain later. Don't shoot, though."

Chatty, terribly out of breath but less scared of a heart attack than a cow, ran toward his friends. "Shoot! Shoot! What are you waiting for?"

Sanders hollered, "We're prohibited from shooting these feral cows. Run to the front porch and up the steps. Quickly." Then, turning again to Pepper, Sanders explained, "It's near impossible for a cow to climb steps. It's pretty laborious for their large bodies."

"It may be too laborious for Chatty," Stella joked.

Then, reaching the top of the steps, Chatty stopped, the cow, indeed, deterred by the steps and standing at the bottom. "A cow?" He said with absolutely no belief. "That wild animal is a cow chasing me through the wilderness?"

Pepper was bent over, doubled with laugher. Stella, practically choking with laughter she was holding back, turned her back so Chatty couldn't see the immense joy she was having. She even pulled the broad brim of her hat over her face to hide the well-deserved grin. However, if she had stopped to think, she would have remembered that Chatty did not laugh during her debacle at the Buckhead Country Club when she was in trouble. But, then again, Chatty did bring up the occasion, incessantly, making digs here and there. So, she felt a little better having the enjoyment.

Chatty stood in the entranceway to the mansion, partially hiding behind the front door, while the cow, looking downright pitiful, remained at the bottom of the steps mourning "the prey that had escaped." He tried to climb the steps, but they were too narrow. The poor thing bawled like a cow who'd had had its baby calf taken away and this, now, broke Stella's heart as she had remembered well, on the farm, how cows would low sadly for days when their baby was taken away—to place in another pasture or to be sold. Chatty, who was slowly beginning to reclaim his arrogance, replied, "Oh, go ahead, Mr. US Marshal, laugh about an American citizen who barely escaped being torn to pieces by a savage beast."

The cow, having cried enough and having had time to think, started again to climb the steps.

Calmly, Pepper walked toward the "wild beast" who had nearly claimed Chatty's life. Putting his gun back in its holster, he raised his hands. The cow stopped and looked at Pepper a moment, offered a loud moo, followed by a mad clod off the step, then finally made a hard gallop back to his abode.

Chapter Fifteen

❧

Pepper and Sanders enjoyed a cold Coke while sitting on the low, white-painted wall that edged the yard, at the bottom side of the lawn that encased the large rectangle pool. "How did cows get here?"

Sanders took a sip and swallowed. "A couple of theories, at least. One is that they were originally domestic cows that swam over from Darien."

"That's a long swim."

Sanders nodded, taking another sip of Coke. "Yeah, but remember all those Westerns where they're driving cows across the wild country? There're a lot of cows swimming in those movies where they have to cross rivers. Actually, cows are quite good swimmers and can swim for miles."

Pepper was shaking his head in disbelief. "I don't understand why cows would just suddenly take off in a herd or in two's and three's and swim this far. What's the other theory?"

Sanders drained his Coke. "This one makes more sense to me. Reynolds had them brought over for milk and butter. I think I even heard that he liked buttermilk. He was, after all, from the upper part of North Carolina and his daddy came from Virginia—so he might have been a buttermilk lover. Bottom line is that my opinion is Reynolds brought them over. He needed to spend his money somehow." Sanders laughed, adding, " As if mansions, yachts, planes, and antiques weren't enough."

About that time, they looked up to see Stella, still wearing her hat—now with her sunglasses placed atop the brim.

"Whew. Chatty is still shaking. He wanted me to give him a Xanax, but the Governor had already poured him a shot of brandy that must be a hundred years old, at least. It's all we could find. Cager said, 'Don't spit it out. Take it like a man.'"

Those were not the words to say to Chatty since he was scared of his own shadow and was used to having no drama in his life. Chatty took the drink and, as the country song goes, "his eyes bugged out and his face turned blue." After three or four seconds, it was obvious, he wouldn't spit it out though it was close-going for a bit.

Inside the mansion, Chatty was still responding to the shot he'd just tossed back.

"Oh, my! That was most unpleasant. I would rather that cow had bitten me."

"Chatham, you overexaggerate," the Governor responded.

"Who? Me?" Chatty, though having been told that many times, was still surprised. "I am the paramount of truth and fact."

Before the Governor could reply, Stella, Pepper, and Sanders walked in as Sanders said, "I told them that we are having dinner with Miss Ginger at eight. She's making green noodles and shrimp that everyone loves. It's a recipe from a now-gone restaurant on St. Simons. So, we better get to investigating."

The men returned to the basement, where they joined Joseph, while Chatty fell back, prostrate, on the sofa, one leg hanging off the side.

"Can someone bring me a bag with ice in it?" he called. But no one replied. Sitting up, Chatty talked to himself, "Some kind of friends I have. Especially Stella. She should be sitting right here, holding my hand and weeping softly over the near loss of her best friend. I surely shan't make it through this." Then, the brandy, still potent after a hundred years, dropped him off, into a dead sleep, as he fell back on the couch.

Stella, meanwhile, wandered from room to room, carefully examining everything she could when, suddenly, a thought hit her: Where were the suspects? The witnesses, if there were any. She had just made it to a bedroom that, curiously, had two in/out doors. One was in the traditional place and the other at the side of the bathroom.

"How strange," she thought, then chalked it up to a rich man's eccentricites.

But with the thought of the witnesses, she raced down the nearest staircase into a den, through the living room, and to the door leading down the deadly stairs.

"Hey, you expert investigators," she called from the top. "Does anyone know where the possible witnesses and suspects might be?"

Sheriff Goudelock then explained that they were all sequestered, across the river, at the hotel, The Oaks on the River. There were seven of them. Twelve others, who had been there that weekend, had taken the last ferry home several hours before the incident. Seven executives, including Spencer, had stayed on the island to discuss deeper matters. The Sheriff and GBI had five officers in total, three interviewing the individuals, while two Deputies stood, watchful, at either ends of the hall.

"We questioned them that night but, not at length. They spent the night here since we had planned more questioning for the next day. Before I could arrive, the Governor called so we made arrangements at the hotel where they were happy to oblige. No one wanted to stay in this house after that."

Just then, a thin, unsure voice called from upstairs. "Is anyone down there?"

The Governor and Sheriff looked to the top of the stairs where stood the skinniest, tallest man they had ever seen. Pepper had already met him. He was African American, with dark hair cut close to his head. He wore a cheap, white shirt, a paisley tie that his mother gave him a month ago for his birthday, dark britches, and black loafers, scuffed and well-worn. What he wore was inexpensive, but it was very respectful to the job. McCager liked that enormously. Too many kids wear casual clothes to work, he thought. At the Burnetts' bank, the executives had made a terrible misjudgment. In fact, McCager had been in his bank a year or so earlier on "Casual Friday". He stamped, with great purpose, over to the bank President's assistant and asked, "Is George in?"

"Yes, sir, Governor," she (who was dressed in blue jeans, a white tee shirt and red cardigan), replied. "He's on the phone but he will want to know you're here. I'll slip him a note."

Within 60 seconds of the assistant emerging from the President's office, the President himself hurried out. "Governor! What an honor to see you." They shook hands. "Would you like to step in my office?"

The Governor produced the smile he had learned in politics. Not a smile he meant but one that appeared that he meant it. In the office, George Harris shut the door. "Please, have a seat."

McCager shook his head. "No need to sit. This won't take long."

George swallowed. He knew McCager Burnett, and this didn't sound good.

"George," he began in a stern voice. "I've been an attorney for forty-five years and a politician nearly as long. And every day, without fail, I have worn a suit and tie. Should I choose to dress casually, in appropriate settings such as a picnic, I might wear a sports jacket without a tie. The way you dress shows how much respect you have for your business. I've always had plenty of respect for my work and my clients. I have respect for my money. It took a lot of hours to earn and a lot of hours away from Miss Alva. I expect *you* to respect my money."

"Yes, sir."

McCager pointed out to the lobby where the casually dressed staff of tellers, customer service reps, and loan account representatives looked as if they were at a ballgame. "If I come in here again and see people dressed liked this, in a bank where Miss Alva and I have our money, I will sign the papers that day to move my financial matters to an institution that respects a person's money, whether they have a little or a lot. And they don't wear yard clothes to work."

George was suddenly shaking. This was not good news. McCager Burnett was one of the most influential men in the state. And not only that, since the Governor was no longer in politics, he now served on the board of the bank. In short, this was trouble that had to be dealt with.

"Sir, I understand completely and it will be handled. Immediately."

"See that it is." McCager started to the door. With his hand on the doorknob, he turned around and said slyly, "I'll be back next Friday," he winked. "And, please, tell your lovely wife 'hello' for me." Then off went Tornado McCager Burnett.

McCager was not even out of the bank, as George could see from his glass-fronted office, before George had his Executive Vice President on the phone. "Casual Fridays are canceled as of today and I charge you with making the announcement at the officers' meeting on Monday morning after which they can tell their subordinates." George listened for a moment. "Why? Two words—McCager Burnett. Enough said. Thank you."

That would explain why the Governor liked Joseph Maycomb upon first sight. Later, he would come to like him much more for other reasons.

As for Joseph, he had met a man who would prove to be a mentor for many years to come.

Chapter Sixteen

☙

As Sanders was putting Stella and Pepper on the DNR boat that had been arranged for them, in order to make their way to the hotel to interview the witnesses and possible suspects, he handed them raincoats.

Grinning, he said," These little boats have a spray to them that the ferry doesn't. Pull up your hoods and tie them tight."

And away they went.

Before they left, however, they had spoken to Joseph Maycomb. With no fanfare or attitude, he laid out evidence on the large, steel preparation table in the kitchen after he had sterilized it well. After Mr. Rascal had left the office and warned him to get some sleep, the energy of youth kicked in and he went to work, digging deeper into the evidence they had.

He had pictures, charts, graphs, and his brain—as smart as any that either Stella or Pepper had encountered.

"Marshal, there's just no way that it could have been accidental."

Pepper looked at him and raised his light brown eyebrows. "You mean, in your opinion."

Jospeh looked at him for a moment, thinking how his Mama would've expected him to answer. She taught him self-confidence as well as respect. The two men looked eye-to-eye, then Jospeh spoke.

"No, sir. I try not to have opinions. I aim to stick to the facts and evidence. And this is what the evidence shouts out, clearly."

Pepper and Stella smiled at the young man who was almost half their age. Unexplainably, they had confidence in him. Joseph took off big, black-frame glasses and tucked them into his pocket. He folded his arms and looked at them. "I'll take any question you have."

Pepper nodded. "Is there any way that, as Mr. Houghton neared the bottom of the stairs, there could have been a bump, sort of a toss-up in the air where he hit the beam?"

Joseph removed a pencil from his plastic pocket protector which his daddy had given him, then took a piece of paper and drew the scene as he saw it. Mr. Houghton, at about 6'1", was most likely standing straight. At any rate, his shoulders were slumped forward, just a bit. He opened the door—or possibly someone else opened the door—and Houghton was turned, facing the stairs.

"How do you know he was standing, facing the stairs," Stella asked, studying Joseph's rather professional drawing. "By the way, you'd make a good artist."

He smiled then said, "I thought about it, but the draw of medical science was too strong a pull. But to answer your question, had Mr. Houghton gone backwards, he would have hit the back of his head, not his forehead. See, in a narrow space like this, and it's much narrower than our modern-day staircases, it would be nigh to impossible for him to flip. He was too big for that."

"Nigh," Stella said softly to herself. "It sounds like something that dear Cager would say."

"Let me ask you this," Pepper said. "Can you tell if it took the strength of a man to push him or could a woman have done it?"

"Either. Even a child could push him, but it wouldn't have been with the force of this fall. My theory is that his forehead hit the beam so hard that his head snapped back hard and broke his neck. Then, he hit the stairs with such force that it broke his back. The various cuts and bruises on his face, most likely, came when his face hit the cement. Now, it's possible that a part of this theory isn't right but I'm almost certain that this is how it happened."

Stella asked, "Then, what about the crystal highball glass that he was holding as he fell? Was he cut by any of that glass?"

"With the measurements I took from where the body was, and then from where the glass was found, I'd say no. Just like a bullet, shattered glass has a velocity it travels with. My theory..." he chuckled, continuing, "You'll be tired of hearing the words 'my theory'. My sweet Mama declares that my first words were 'my theory'."

He shook his head with a kind expression that proved who Joseph Maycomb was. Then, returning to what he'd been saying a moment earlier, "I'm surprised he held onto the glass as long as he did. But sometimes, when we're scared or uncertain, we need to cling to something. That was probably true with Mr. Houghton. He held on to it until, at last, it was knocked out of his hand."

Joseph paused and looked at Stella and Pepper. "Any guess when that would have been?"

"When his head hit the beam," Stella replied quickly.

"That's right—his hand would have popped opened, kind of an instant-reflex to the hit."

Pepper looked at the ravishing beauty with admiration. She was smart, beautiful, kind, and hard working. She was the most perfect woman he had ever met, even more than his mother and he had always thought that no one could be more beautiful and certainly not as kind. Suddenly, something occurred to him. Maybe that's why he couldn't commit. No one was as good as his mother. Not the boloney that the doctor fed him after his shootout, about having PTSD, and having an inability to commit. He studied her with admiration.

"Well, we might have to make you a US Marshal," Pepper finally said, smiling. She was proud of herself, and Pepper's compliment made her even prouder.

Joseph tapped the pencil on the desk and said, "Absolutely. Correct. Miss Stella, it's simply the reflex of the body."

"Joseph, when we got there, there was the faintest whiff of Jack Daniel's Black Label liquor. Would the smell have lingered? I definitely could smell it after a couple of days."

He rolled his eyes. "You should have been here that night. It was definitely high volume."

"Could it have smelled like that on the concrete floor for so long?"

"For a while—but not as long as it has been now. The wood on the steps picked it up, though.

Stella thought of something. "I'm not a whiskey drinker but Pepper had a glass the other night. Now, that's one of the more expensive Jack Daniel's. Is that correct?"

"Oh, yeah," Pepper replied. "Sometimes, when I'm with Chatty, I feel the need for something 'top shelf' to get me through!"

"Chatty?" Joseph had never heard of such a name. In Sparta, people would laugh at the name which goes to show there is a point for everyone to giggle about someone else. Because snooty Chatty would have turned up his nose at the boarded town of Sparta and the convenience store with the iron bars on the window. The one where Joseph's mother had worked for fifteen years.

Pepper motioned the question away with his hand, saying, "Never mind. You'll meet him soon enough. But let me warn you that nothing your good Mama in Sparta, Georgia, ever taught you has prepared you for Chatham Balsam Colquitt, IV. That is, 'Chatty'." He looked pointedly at Stella who smiled then said, somewhat sheepishly, "He's my best friend."

Pepper rolled his eyes. To be honest, Chatty was starting to get on Pepper's nerves because he was getting between himself and Stella. At first, it wasn't bad. But now, every day, it was a little harder on Pepper. A little more of an annoyance.

"I was looking through the rooms in the mansion," Stella said, getting back to the subject at hand. "And as I wandered about, I kept noticing a slight smell. At first, I thought it was just the smell of an old house—but then I realized it was a smell I knew but couldn't place. It was so faint. But this conversation just brought it to mind—it's Jack Daniel's Black Label."

"Are you sure?" Pepper asked.

She nodded firmly, her gold hoop earrings swinging back and forth. "Positive."

Pepper put his arm around her shoulders. "Stella, dear, Stella, there is no way you could smell it in every room. It's faded significantly in the basement. You must have just imagined it."

That red-headed fury that Stella could have, time to time—though she did manage it better than most red heads—sprang up hard and stunningly fast. She shook her head and the anger unraveled from the top of her red hair all the way to her orange Kate Spade shoes.

"Jackson Culpepper, how dare you patronize me AND question me after all we've been through." She stomped her foot so hard that it hurt, then put her hands on her hips. "I'm not some dumb mountain girl who doesn't have enough sense to know the difference between the smell of an old house and a high-priced whiskey. Give me some credit. I learned some things by being married to Asher Bankwell!"

Pepper jumped back noticeably. He had never seen this side of Stella and, prayed to God, that he never would again. "Whoa. Stella. Calm down. Please. I didn't mean to upset you. But the smell of whiskey throughout the house? This very big, old house?"

She folded her arms and looked away to the side. She looked like a perfect Barbie doll, having a fuss with Ken. "I'm more convinced than ever."

Joseph looked at Pepper and shrugged his shoulders in a "What're you gonna do?" fashion.

Pepper sighed and reached over to take Stella's hand. A bold move, had it been romantic, but this wasn't.

"Why don't you take me through all the rooms you've been through and let me see... or smell," Pepper said, trying to joke. Stella turned to Pepper.

"You don't trust me!" she pressed her mouth together in an angry pout.

Pepper, a personable, charming guy, had learned the best way to turn an angry situation was to play along. In a humorous tone, he said, "It could be, *could be*, that its Jack Daniel's Master Distiller Series. A bottle of that costs hundreds of dollars and we know that Houghton could afford it. Will you, please, show me around? I know how smart you are. I'm not doubting you for one second of one Elvis song."

She laughed. He had already figured out how much she loved Elvis. Appeased and tamed, still holding his hand, she said, "Come with me," pulling him forward, behind her. "They passed into the front room. Pepper sniffed the air.

Smelling nothing, he went over to one of the beige loveseats and sat down.

"Hmmmm…" then suddenly, he said, "I do smell it."

Stella folded her arms and gave him an I-told-you-so look then offered a proud smile to Joseph who had appropriately tagged along. Stella really was pleased with herself. She had learned that affectation, of being pleased with oneself, from Chatty.

Pepper picked up one of the sofa pillows. "Whoa!" he exclaimed, "I certainly smell it now!"

He moved to the fireplace but didn't smell it there. Then, over to the other love seat where a small hint of it lifted from the fabric.

Joseph then curiously asked, "Is it only on the fabric? Materials obviously hold scents and smells much longer." As Pepper, Stella, and, now Joseph, began furiously smelling the furniture in various rooms, they discovered good ol 'Jack Daniel's Black on every fabric. And in every room that followed.

"Oh, that's a drunk man for sure," Pepper said. Joseph, raised in a strict teetotaling family, was absolutely no help here. Pepper was the expert and Stella did have an impressive sense of smell, especially after she had spent some time visiting Asher's home bar, sneaking a shot or two during their hellacious last year. Blindfold Stella, put any high brand of whiskey in front of her, and she could tell it was whiskey, even with her limited knowledge—especially after the party ended and Asher came to bed, even though he had showered, she could smell the whiskey. This was where she first discovered his affair with Annabelle. She had smelled her perfume on his shirt and, the next night, smelled it again, swirling about, after a high-society party Asher and she had attended.

Right about then, Sanders appeared. "The boat's ready and we need to go because some rough waves are coming in."

"We just need to run downstairs and talk briefly to the Governor and Sheriff. Do we have ten minutes?"

"Yes," Sanders replied, "but not eleven minutes. These small boats can be ticklish in bad water. I hate to have any more deaths this week."

On the way to the kitchen, Stella let out a small cry. "Chatty! Where is he? He was on the sofa."

So, that took them on a scavenger hunt where, finally, Chatty was discovered, passed-out from the brandy (apparently a very good and strong year), curled up on a velvet-covered banquette that went halfway around the table.

"Why did he move in here and how was he even able to get up?" Stella's mind could never stop.

"Leave him be," Pepper instructed. "The Governor can take care of him. We've got to get across the water and it'll be dark, soon."

In ten quick minutes, they explained to the Sheriff and Governor what had happened and about the smell. Joseph suggested, "I'll see if I can get some residual scent from the fabric".

With goodbyes said, Stella, Pepper and Sanders ran for the truck as twilight was falling. There was a flash of lightning.

Back at the Reynolds' mansion, the Governor was asking the Sheriff, "Now, what in the tarnation do you think all this whiskey means? It's baffling."

"Governor," Goudelock replied, "I think it's more than bafflin'. I think it may be unexplainable."

To any law man, that's the worst phrase that can be uttered.

Chapter Seventeen

ⵣ

Carlie, who had made the arrangements for the sequestered group, since she was in charge of reservations for the hotel, met Pepper and Stella and was such a joyful soul that it took an edge off the grimness of the situation.

Carlie showed them to the conference room where she, kindly and thoughtfully, had put out cold drinks and snacks.

"Is there anything else I can do to help?" she asked.

"Would you mind giving us a list of the rooms each person's in?" Pepper purposely avoided using the word "suspect." He didn't want to alarm Carlie any more than she already must be, with all the GBI agents and Deputies. And the fact that some were wearing bulletproof vests didn't ease the tension. Carlie opened a black leather notebook and pulled out a carefully compiled sheet. "I thought you might need it," she said, handing the paper to Pepper. It was exactly what he needed. At the moment.

Pepper shook his head in surprise, appreciation and admiration. "Carlie, you should run the country. You're amazing. Thank you!"

Her smile showed her gratitude for the compliment. "If you don't need anything else, I'll take leave." Then, handing

Pepper her business card, she said, "This has my cell number but I do expect to be on property for a few more hours. My office is the first door on the left, just past the registration. Will y'all be needing rooms tonight?"

"I don't think so," said Pepper. "We plan to go back to the island and stay in a couple of cottages they have there for us. Thank you for your help. You've made everything a lot easier."

After Carlie left, Pepper showed Stella the list. "Any thoughts on who we should speak to first?"

"It's a guess but let's bring Kyle Kirby in." As usual, Stella's instincts would not fail her.

When Kirby arrived, introductions were made, and Kirby accepted a bottle of water. Stella settled in a comfortable purple velvet chair while Kirby and Pepper sat down on a brightly-colored green velvet love seat. Kirby was about 5'2", as wide as he was tall, dressed casually, even apologizing that he wasn't wearing a suit or tie.

"It was a corporate retreat so Spencer said we could dress casually." Kirby cleared his throat and swallowed. Having said Spencer's name, he choked up.

"You liked Spencer?" Stella asked with compassion in her voice.

He nodded, fighting back tears. "He was kind to me. Once, when I was on an international business trip, a virus broke out in that country so authorities closed the border. Spencer made certain my wife and children were taken care of back home. He even sent dinner over every night. A good man. Really good."

Stella and Pepper looked at each other. They had to be careful not to be tricked by someone who pretended to love Spencer yet may not have. On the other hand, they had to give him the benefit of doubt.

"Mr. Kirby," Pepper began.

"Call me Kyle. It'll make me less nervous." He smiled weakly.

"Kyle, will you tell us about that night, starting with the last afternoon?"

Kyle thought for a moment, either gathering his thoughts or preparing his lies. "We had an agenda which was already on our bed when we arrived. It had been a good conference. That afternoon, we finished about 4 o'clock. Twelve who were in attendance were released to take the last ferry and return home."

"Why were the other seven who were left chosen to stay?" asked Stella. "That's right, isn't it?" Stella was smart enough to play a bit dumb. She knew, without question, that seven, in addition to Spencer, remained at the Reynolds House.

"I can't speak for all of them. That seemed odd to me. Like a couple of assistants—Spencer's and Ance's—because we were finished with work. But, at least, I thought I was asked to stay because I'm in charge of investor relations. We have a stockholders meeting coming up and Spencer discussed that. He was concerned by a shareholder who had been on a rampage about dividends which we had cut by 50 percent."

"That's quite a cut!" softly exclaimed Stella who had always watched the dividends when she and Asher were married. Once, she had asked him about their Coca-Cola stock because the dividends were always modest.

"It's a blue chip stock—that means its stock value is solid in good times and bad. We plunge money back into the company and through acquisitions, like water. When consumers stopped drinking as much Coke but more water, we bought a water company years before the trend of everyone toting around bottles of it. Brilliant move. The stock price itself stays steady. The dividends always come back. Even when they drop during a quarter, they'll be back at a higher price by the next quarter. Don't worry."

Stella had nodded. She always believed Asher. It is useless to mention that's how she got herself in trouble in the first place. Too, his father, Jasper, had been a longtime board member of the Coke corporation. As a result, no Bankwell money was allowed to be spent on anything but Coke products. Since their separation, Stella had continued to buy Coke products, and even water, and she now possessed a sizable share of that company's stock, thanks to her divorce agreement. Should she ever be in a restaurant and order a Coke only to hear "We have Pepsi. Is that alright?" she was always quick to reply, "I'll just have water, then. No ice, please."

"Why was Malachi stock cut so severely?" she asked.

"A few reasons. New equipment that was needed in plants. The patent on one of our most popular pharmaceuticals expired so generic versions came out and insurance companies began insisting their patients use them, instead. Now, for some people, the generic doesn't work as well so the insurance companies have to allow the insured to use our original pharmaceutical. But let's face it, there's a big difference between paying a co-pay of ten dollars or paying a co-pay of sixty dollars for virtually the same drug. Those kinds of things are big hits for us, hits that we're still reeling from."

"But you know those hits are coming," Stella pressed. "You probably know for several years in advance. A company is aware when its patents expire."

"Of course," he replied. But Kyle was taken aback. He didn't expect to run into someone so savvy in financial business. He figured Stella was just the Marshal's pretty partner. After Asher, Stella had become a faithful reader of the *Wall Street Journal*. She'd learned so much from Asher's crimes and now that she was on her own, she had to do the best she could with what money she had so she read the financials religiously. However, Kyle had answered in such a terse way that she knew there had to be more to the story.

"Did Spencer know?" It was a preposterous question. He was CEO of the company.

Kyle suddenly was not so friendly. "He knew when patents were expiring."

"Did he know the grave effect it would have on the company? Did he know how it would affect the profits? Had you kept him informed, accurately, about all of that?"

Kyle did not speak. He looked at Stella with disdain— not meant for Stella but, rather, for the long-gone Spencer.

Pepper saw this and stepped in. "We need to ask these questions, Mr. Kirby, but let me explain something. When you're hesitant to answer, it doesn't look good." He paused and a slight, wicked smile came to his face. "In fact, it looks very bad. Now, the truth, please."

Kyle's shoulders slumped. He looked defeated. "Spencer never bothered with the numbers. He trusted everybody. He was a decent businessman, but he was distracted by the fun his money could buy, like month-long trips to Italy. The board was content to let him do that as long as they were getting healthy dividend checks. There *is* one board member, Minton Armstrong, who's on the board because he owns a very successful cosmetics company. This has been particularly helpful in showing the company how to understand women since we've come out with this highly successful diet drug. Minton's background is as an accountant. And... he started snooping around when Spencer was in Paris, playing with his girlfriend. Minton called for an audit and, since he was Vice Chairman and Spencer was out of the country, he had the authority."

Finally, they were getting good information. More people are killed over money than love.

"What happened with the audit?" Pepper asked, completely humorless.

"I got caught. What I'd done was enough to put us in trouble with the Feds and put me, and possibly other members of the company, in prison. I doctored the numbers."

"When did Spencer learn about this?"

Kyle Kirby started weeping, quietly. "Spencer's been nothing but good to me and I betrayed him."

Kirby went on to explain that he didn't know that Spencer was aware of anything until they all got to Sapelo. Still, he didn't know until the other twelve employees left. After an afternoon dessert snack, the others adjourned to their rooms until cocktails before dinner. They'd planned to leave the next day. As the group was breaking up, Spencer had said, "Hey, Kyle, I'd like to speak to you a moment, if you don't mind." He said it very casually.

"Just like that—my life was about to be destroyed yet he was so cool about it." Kirby said it with a sense of wonderment as he looked up to the ceiling.

However, it was agreed by all who knew Spencer that he was exceedingly kind and courteous to everyone. No one had ever seen him be rude or even mildly snappish. Perhaps it was just his personality. But this was the question that Stella and Pepper would debate over the next day: was Spencer that kind or that cold-hearted? He had taken Kyle into the den.

Spencer walked over to the cart that served as a bar, picked up a Waterford crystal decanter, glistening like a diamond as the afternoon sun streamed in through the high, arched window and bounced its rays off the fine glass. Kyle recalled that he was mesmerized by the dancing light.

"Whiskey?" he asked as he poured half a glass for himself. "Jack Daniel's Black. It's all I drink unless I go into the really expensive stuff."

Kirby shook his head. "I don't really drink much anymore. I'll occasionally drink wine but never more than once a week."

Spencer walked over and sat down in a large, leather chair. He had known Kyle Kirby for years and he had never known that about him. "Really? I never knew anyone to have a disciplined schedule like that."

"History of addiction in my family. Long before anyone had a name for it. I don't want to give it free reign in my life."

"Good for you. I admire that." Spencer twirled the glass around, studying the pattern cut into it. "Interesting men Jack Daniel and R.J. Reynolds. They both made their fortunes in the very thing that killed them. Tobacco did in Reynolds and Daniel died from gangrene after kicking the safe in his office, trying to get to his whiskey money." Spencer fell into deep thought, staring at a vase. "I have friends in Tennessee that say that he gave money to a church he didn't attend. Then, one day, listening to a sermon outside the church window, something caught hold of him and zap, from then on, he called himself a Christian." Spencer gave a small laugh. "He got baptized in the very same river water he used to make his whiskey. Now, there's a story, right?"

Kirby was growing anxious. He'd known Spencer Houghton for twenty years, but he'd never seen him make this kind of small talk. There was a long silence in the room as Kirby fiddled with a button on his gray, cashmere cardigan. Kirby looked around at the artwork, then to the bookcase where he noticed a volume, *Theodore Roosevelt: The Roosevelt*

Family of Sagamore Hill. Trying to break the tension, he commented, \"It's interesting to look at a man's bookshelf, seventy or eighty years after they die, and know what he was reading. It gives you real insight into that person."

Kyle pointed to the book. "Theodore Roosevelt. I can see how Richard Reynolds would like him. They were men who enjoyed life with strong enthusiasm and —"

"Kirby, I have to fire you," Spencer suddenly blurted out.

Stella asked, since she had taken over the interview without any resistance from Pepper, "How did that make you feel?"

After a long moment, Kirby finally replied, "I went through a wheel of emotions. My version of the stages of grief. First, I was stunned. I had no indication. Three months ago, we moved into a new house where my mortgage is three times what it was in the other house—a house which was $40,000 away from being paid off. Spencer knew about it and even had to sign papers verifying my salary and employment. Then, I went from hurt, to disbelief, to upset, to being anxious over how I was going to tell my wife." He stopped. And then, after another long moment, admitted, "I cried." He dropped his head into his hands. Sadly, he shook his head, looking all the while at the floor and said, "I haven't cried since my Granddaddy died fifteen years ago. I thought I had used up all the tears God gave me until the day that Spencer, one of the finest men I ever knew, said to me, so casually, 'I have to fire you.'" Kirby took some time to collect his emotions, then eventually continued.

"It finally added up to anger. Really dark, black anger. I'll admit that to you even though I know it will make me a suspect. The truth always comes out anyway, so I'll just lay my cards on the table."

Pepper leaned in closely. "Did you hate Houghton enough to kill him?"

Stella did think that that was a bit rude. She might be mountain born and raised but she knew better, and Pepper did get a quick glance at Stella's look of surprise then disapproval. "Note to self," Pepper thought, "Explain to Stella how investigations work."

Immediately, he needed her to be the good guy and charm the folks while Pepper had plenty of experience with being the black hat. And, if he got into a bind, he could always count on McCager Burnett. There was no two ways about it. Cager could play the bad guy in an investigation as well as Pepper. Of course, he had had a lot more years of experience—not to mention all those years in Washington. That'll turn any man tough.

Kyle Kirby surprised both of them with his answer. He clasped his hands and leaned forward, his elbows resting on a pair of navy slacks and raised his head. Stella, ever observant, with a photographic memory, recalled something she had glanced in an upstairs bedroom that day. It was on a shelf, under a table, beside a bed. It was a black hat with an unusually wide brim. Since it was about the size of the sun hat that she was wearing, she thought nothing of it at the time. But now, her mind started clicking.

Once, when she was working press for the Cleveland Grand Prix, she and a couple of friends went out to an Amish community and saw how they lived—no electricity, no motor vehicles, and some of the most delicious food she'd ever tasted, not to mention the amazing respect each had for one another. Men wore gray or black and the women, always subservient to their husbands, worked as hard as the men making bread, cakes, pie, jellies and custard that their families could eat and that they could sell from roadside stands.

One of Stella's co-workers had remarked, "They probably make more in one month than I make in a year."

"I could certainly get used to life without Internet and, though I'd miss re-runs of *My Three Sons* and *That Girl*, I could live without TV," Stella had replied. "I'd just read all the time," and this she said dreamily, "the same way I did when I wandered the hills and creeks back home, when I was growing up. I always had a book in my hands."

Stella's mind clicked a bit further back. There was something else out of place in that bedroom but what was it? "That's it!" she said quietly. "A flat screen TV was missing. The outline where it had been was there but the paint on the wall where it once hung was a darker color. At the time, she assumed it was out for repair. Or being replaced. Aw, but the hat and the missing television now made sense. Kyle had asked for the TV to be removed. She stood up, smoothing her orange dress.

"Pepper, would you mind if I sat beside Mr. Kirby?" Pepper looked stunned and didn't move. Then, she spoke up with a comic delivery. "Hop to it, Culpepper. Didn't your Mama teach you to stand when a lady stands?" Wickedly, she grinned. "Just be glad that Chatty's still suffering the effects of hundred-year-old whiskey or, boy, would he be reciting from *What Southern Gentlemen Know (That Every Man Should)*. He keeps that book on his nightstand and travels with it always in his luggage. Now, if he read the Bible like he reads that book, we'd have another Billy Graham on our hands."

"No, we wouldn't," replied Pepper, standing up and stepping aside, then walking over to stand across the room, leaving the end of the sofa open, for Stella. "Chatty would never live in a log cabin," Pepper quipped showing that he knew where the famed preacher and his family had lived on a mountain in North Carolina—and surprising Stella. Graham's log cabin had been Pepper's assigned duty a couple of times when distinguished officers from abroad, as well as from the US, were visiting Rev. Graham.

When Stella moved to the edge of the sofa, next to Kyle, he courteously stood up.

Stella glanced at Pepper. "See? A perfect gentleman. Chatty would approve."

Kyle sat back down and was still as Stella smoothed her dress underneath herself and sat. "Chatty?" he asked bewildered. "I don't know what you—"

"You haven't met him," Pepper said, flipping through a Golden Isles magazine that was laying on the table. "And, if fortune smiles on you, you never will." He said it casually and not with unkindness. Just frank, honest talk.

Stella then put a sympathetic hand on Mr. Kirby's chair but instinctively knew not to touch as all Southerners are apt to do. She leaned close toward him, her gold bangles, each a different size, making the only sound in the room.

"Kyle, do you mind if I ask you something? And, please, know that this is for purpose of finding out how Mr. Houghton died."

Kirby nodded. There were no tears in his eyes, only the saddest expression she'd ever seen on anyone's face.

"Are you Amish?"

Pepper looked up from the *Golden Isles* magazine, pausing, with page in hand.

Kirby nodded yes.

Wordlessly, Stella turned to Pepper and said easily, "I don't believe Kyle could have killed Mr. Houghton. The Amish are peaceful people who believe, devoutly, in serving with forgiveness for their fellow man."

Relief drifted over Kirby. "How did you know?" he asked softly.

"When I was rambling through the mansion, I saw your hat on the shelf beneath the nightstand. Do you always travel with it?"

He sighed. "Yes. I forgot it when I left and I've been worrying all afternoon how I was going to get it back. It reminds me of my home, of where I come from." He shook his head sadly and said, "I've failed my parents. My entire family is ashamed of me."

"You're so successful."

"That's why. It's our custom that we're allowed to go out, into the world as teenagers, to see if we choose the world or the Amish. Once we've chosen, however, we can't turn back. After my time in the world, I chose Amish because I knew that was what my father wanted. I always tried to please him. But, after I was baptized into the Amish church, I couldn't quit thinking about the outside world. I knew I had made a mistake. So, two years after I'd made my commitment, I left again. It meant leaving behind my family, the girl I loved, a life full of simple pleasures and kind living, forever." He played with his watch—something else the Amish disapproved of, and added, "It's the kind of decision on which I wish I had waited, and it would never have happened."

Stella turned to Pepper. "Regardless of how mad Kyle was at Mr. Houghton, he's had a lifetime of teaching to forgive. One of the greatest sins in the Amish community is anger."

Pepper looked at Stella and shook his head. "How did you figure that out?"

"In the mountains, we're taught to be observant of everything: a squirrel scrambling up a tree, a look of pain in a horse's eyes, how the leaves on a tree blow backwards when a storm is coming. I don't always stop and process the minute I see something, but it certainly sticks in the back of my mind."

Pepper squeezed her hand and smiled. An inch more of love had squeezed into his heart. She smiled back and his heart felt like it melted into a puddle. He snapped out of it.

"Kyle, since we've not clearly established you as not being a suspect (because cynical Pepper had thought it possible that Kirby was playing them) would you answer some other questions?"

"Of course."

"Did Mr. Houghton and your co-workers know that you're Amish?"

He shook his head. "For that, I'm ashamed, too, when Mr. Houghton fired me. I have given up everything to work my way up, through a company like this. It has hurt in my heart all these years, but I have always satisfied myself by thinking I was doing right by my wife and children. I have two daughters still in college. And, as I said, buying a house far beyond what we can afford as well as a vacation house on the gulf coast. Sending my kids to high-priced colleges, having them drive expensive cars. I've been so unthinking. And unkind." He lifted his head from his hands and looked at Stella, tears streaming down his face. "I did take my family to church. An interdenominational church but it's a long way from the kind of church I grew up in. My family wouldn't approve of that, either." He shook his head. "What a bind I'm in. Unfixable, I'm afraid."

As she listened, Stella, was thinking back to what her own father, Sims, would say, 'You sell a bit of your soul to the devil just once and he never stops a'comin' back for more.

And, each time, he's willin' to pay a higher price to suit himself. Then, one day, he'll pull the rug out from under you and laugh. The devil is no friend to anyone but himself.'

"Did you ever tell Mr. Houghton, on the day he was killed, that you were Amish?" Stella asked.

"No. I just angrily explained that I was in a position I couldn't get out of. I'm fifty-six years old. My best work years are behind me."

"Did that affect him?" asked Pepper.

"He offered to pay off everything I owe, including the new house." Mr. Kirby dropped his head back into his hands, sobbing.

Pepper thought it but didn't say it: No murder here. There's no motive.

But Pepper did ask, "When was the last time you saw him?"

"At dinner with Spencer and the rest of us who remained behind. For this first time in my life, I tasted champagne even though I drink wine on occasion. I had a few sips because my nerves needed to be settled. I wanted to go to him and apologize for how harshly I'd spoken. I approached him, timidly, but he said, "You're my friend, Kyle, you'll always be. Remember that. Friendship is different from business. It was the board's decision, not mine."

Kirby bit his lip and thought before speaking further. "Mr. Houghton had a lot to drink. I don't know much about these things, but I think he may have been drunk. He slurred when he talked and had staggered out when leaving the room."

CR

A bit more of useless conversation from Kirby—useless because it was obvious that he had not played a part in Houghton's death. After all, killing someone was the worst thing to the Amish and Kirby was already carrying enough guilt—so they dismissed Kyle, telling him that he could either spend the night at The Oaks or head home. He opted for home since he had driven his car to Darien. Although, it did occur to him that it would be best to take some time before facing his wife. But perhaps, if she saw his great sorrow, she would be more forgiving to learn that she had married a fraud, one who said he had no family and had grown up with an uncle who died when Kyle Kirby was just eighteen. On the other hand, it wasn't a lie. The Amish no longer recognized him as family.

"Keep your phone with you in case we need to check with you on anything," Pepper, said, shaking Kyle's hand. Stella, as usual, was encouraging, "A better day will come. Just get yourself through this, one day at a time.

Quite unusual for someone of Amish upbringing but quite normal for someone who had fallen under the charms of Stella Bankwell, Kyle hugged Stella and thanked her. "Because of you, the Marshal believed me. Thank you."

As soon as Mr. Kirby left the room, Pepper looked at his Timex, with its brown leather band that he had replaced three times, that his grandmother had given him for his college graduation. "It's after seven. Should we order in some dinner or continue to question? It's been a weary day and we still have to get back to the island."

"Let's eat here while we interview a couple more folks, then take the boat to Sapelo. We can come back here for breakfast in the morning and start afresh. I sure was lookin ' forward to Ginger's noodles and shrimp. I'll go to the front desk and call."

Had they only known the kind of night that lay ahead for them on Sapelo, they might have stayed put at The Oaks.

Chapter Eighteen

ঙ

Carlie was still working and, were she to admit it, that was because she wanted to make sure Stella and all the law officers had everything they needed. The officers had eaten in shifts so when Stella went to the front desk to call Ginger, Carlie, notified by the front desk manager, came out of her office.

"Ms. Bankwell, what may I do for you? Would you care to order dinner" Carlie asked.

Stella was so tired that food meant little, but she did ask for a cup of crab chowder and ordered a steak for Pepper because, rarely, did he ever order anything else when they dined together.

She smiled a smile that held an endless well of tiredness. "Would you mind bringing a finger of Jack Daniel's Black to Marshal Culpepper?"

"Of course not!" Carlie said with strong bit of Southern Hospitality. "What else?"

"Well, if you don't mind, I'd like sweet tea." She thought it for a moment. Then, realizing Pepper was "on duty," said to Carlie, "On second thought, Jack Daniel's. Thank you, so much."

As Stella turned to leave, she remembered something and turned back. "Carlie, we'll be interviewing a couple of the guests so think nothing of knocking on the door with the food. You can tell the server." Stella, since she wasn't trained as a law officer, had a different kind of instinct. She didn't follow rules. She followed her gut, and her gut told her that two people eating a late dinner while they talked to the two women, separately that is, would make them more comfortable. Southern women like to see people enjoy food.

"Oh, Lord, please don't let one of these women be a Yankee who can't understand my accent, or a European," Stella said silently as she headed to the conference room. If that were the case, her theory about dinner was all for naught.

Katie Allison Thompson and Martha Martin would add little knowledge to the investigation. Both had been asked by Spencer to stay because they were administrative assistants and might be needed. However, two facts came out that might be a piece of the puzzle. Though interviewed separately, they both had similar bits of information. Mrs. Martin explained that it was because they shared an office outside of Mr. Houghton's so they saw and heard a lot of the same information.

Spencer Houghton, divorced for five years, childless, and among the country's richest men, had, only a week before leaving for Sapelo, broken up with a gold digger named Thea Theressa Olivia Mansford. He had met Theressa through a fraternity brother at Vanderbilt who stayed in Nashville after school. She had once been married to a president of a record label that was rumored to be controlled by the mob, back in the days when real mobs still existed.

Ms. Thompson came first. She was in her mid-thirties, a tiny angel tattoo on the inside of her left wrist, but it was easy to see that she had put make-up on it that day to cover it as much as possible. Her hair was dishwater brown, what Stella's Mama called "stringy"—meaning it was thin and hung ragged on the end. Around her heart-shaped face and to her shoulders, it was thicker, meaning she was wearing a "halo", a hairpiece that was hidden under the teasing atop her scalp and making her hair appear thicker. She was very skinny but hid it well under an olive green, drab suit—a jacket and pencil skirt. Her lipstick was pale, she wore blush and a little eyeshadow, and had no "pop". Nothing of interest stood out. But she was sweet. And, in the South, that matters a lot more than pretty.

She had worked for "Mr. Houghton," as she never failed to call him, for eight years. It was only the second assistant's job she'd had since graduating from business school and moving to New York City for three years. The first was for a man who owned vending machines. He had really made his money in the day when cigarettes were sold in those vending machines. But when legislation put an end to that, he turned to snacks and colas. He was of the old school, New York, lower class business owner: constantly chomping a cigar, using foul language, tough in most ways, kind in others. Finally, Katie moved home to the Delta. She had married briefly while on her New York adventure and what no one could figure was why she kept Thompson as her last name. Her deepest secret was this, though: she hoped that her husband would come looking for her one day and ask her to come back. She still loved him mightily. He knew her hometown, knew that she planned to return there and be rid of New York City, once and for all, but she wanted to make it easy for him to find her.

"Was the break-up between Mr. Houghton and Ms. Manning difficult?" asked Pepper.

"For who?" she replied, smartly, but not in an ugly way. "Him or her?"

Pepper looked down at the table and smiled and Stella looked over at her and winked.

He nodded and said, "Well done. Let me put it this way: for either?"

"Mr. Houghton was still in love with his first wife. He never said an unkind word about her and almost joyfully paid her alimony every month. I'd worked there two or three years before the split so I saw the whole thing. He was heartbroken."

"Another man?"

She shook her head. "It's this simple—and I don't know why people always want it to be more complicated—she just wasn't in love with him. I think she really tried to be in love with him. But she's remarried now and has a baby. I ran into her and her child at the grocery store a couple of months ago. She told me that, even though her alimony payments were supposed to cease when she remarried, Mr. Houghton called

her and said he'd continue paying until one of them died."
Ms. Thompson looked sad. "Imagine being loved like that?"
Ms. Thompson was, of course, thinking of her own husband.

"Now, Thea Theressa Olivia Mansford. Whew. *That*
was ugly."

Stella and Pepper didn't ask then but was told later that
everyone called her by all four names because it was lyrical
and funny. To everyone, she was a joke until the break-up
and then it was no joke.

"In what way?" Stella asked.

"She called countless times a day. She also showed up,
screaming and using unkind language. He tried to keep her
calmed down but to no use."

"Didn't she live in Nashville?"

"Yes, but she took a suite at the Alluvian hotel for days
at the time." Denise, the front desk manager, is the sweetest
woman in the world. I love her to pieces. She would call and
give me the heads-up that Thea Theressa Oliva Mansford was
checking in so Mr. Houghton would go into hiding—usually
down to Biloxi to gamble at the Beau Rivage. I thought the
world of Mr. Houghton. I've cried for two days. I wish I
could give you something that would help you but that's the
best I can do."

"Well, Ms. Thompson, if you think of anything, here's
my card. Please, call."

Mrs. Martin, who had worked for Mr. Houghton for 15
years, had agreed with Ms. Thompson about Thea Theressa
Olivia Mansford's behavior. A senior woman, who was

chubby with hair that was completely silver and who wore glasses, had this to add: "There is one thing you need to know." She unclasped her purse, took out a lace-trimmed handkerchief, and cleared her throat. "As it turns out, Mr. Houghton asked me to stay behind for a precise reason. He said, as kindly as he could, that it was time for me to retire." Tears welled in her eyes.

Stella reached over and patted her shoulder with compassion. "Oh, Mrs. Martin, I'm sorry."

"My husband died ten years ago. Our son lives in St. Louis and our daughter in Memphis. I'm lonely so work gave me a purpose." She started to cry again, the kind of tears that one tries to hold back but can't. "It was hard for Mr. Houghton but the board was pushing him to making changes—like firing Kyle Kirby. I'm afraid I was a terrible baby about it which made him feel worse. He gave me an excellent severance which, I suspect, he was going to pay most from his own pocket." With a cynical grimace, she added, "I suppose I'll never see a penny of that money." Then she shook it off. "That doesn't matter here, though. The world and the state of Mississippi has lost a fine—a very fine—man."

"Did he say why he was letting you go?" asked Pepper, a question which could have gone without being asked, in Stella's opinion, and she kicked him under the table. He barely stopped the word "ouch" from coming out of his mouth in response.

"I'll tell you why," Mrs. Martin said, pulling her shoulders back and holding her head up. "I do shorthand."

Pepper did a double take and asked, "Short what?"

Stella gave him a most aggravated look and he knew he had said something wrong. "Shorthand. It's a brilliant form of coded language. And you'd do well to learn it. It's similar to the telegraph. You have to know the symbols in order to write and read what's written." Stella turned back to Mrs. Martin. "Few are the people who know shorthand these days. I would think that would make you most valuable."

She shrugged and sighed. "Perhaps, if I could also run an IBM computer, it would. But I know nothing about computers. Katie, who was just in here, she's a wiz. She had helped me a lot but I never could learn the programs and I really didn't care to. Two weeks ago, Mr. Houghton's Uncle, the former Chairman of the board but still a powerful board member, came in and saw me in a terrible fix with the computer. I suppose this is how it all happened. Dear, dear Mr. Houghton wouldn't have done it on his own. He valued people over machines and money."

That was that. All either knew. So, the interviews ended for the day.

Half an hour, later Stella and Pepper were climbing onto the boat the DNR had brought for them. Stella, though in a dress, handled her entry onto the boat with grace. There was no talk as they returned to the island because both were holding their hoods closed at the mouth as the cold water flew over them. They arrived back on Sapelo where a truck was waiting to take them to the Reynolds house and then to the cottages where they were staying. The Governor had special permission to stay at the Big House and use Richard Reynolds' room, the one with two doors. And since Chatty had invited himself along, he'd stay at Pepper's three-bedroom cottage.

They walked into the living room and what a sight to behold. The Governor was apparently aggravated, pacing back and forth in front of the fireplace. And Chatham Balsam Colquitt IV?

Chatty was sprawled across the large, red sofa in the front room. He had a wet, white monogrammed handkerchief over his face and a huge ice bag on his head which he held with one hand while the other arm dangled over the back of the sofa. Every few seconds, he heaved heavy, mournful sighs like a big, dying moose. The hapless Governor wore weary on his face like a heavy cloak.

"Thank goodness, y'all are back. I'm worn to a frazzle dealing with this." He pointed a wrinkled finger toward Chatty. "He's all yours now."

Before either Stella or Pepper could say a word, Chatty let out a low moan. Stella, the expert of all things Chatty, went over to her friend.

"Oh, Chatty, please, stop the theatrics. People don't die heavy like this. They die softly because they don't have the strength to carry on the way you are."

Stella snatched the handkerchief from his face, took the ice from his head, and commanded, "Now, sit up. We've got to go to the cottages."

Instantly, Chatty answered her command, sitting up and shaking his head, vigorously.

"Alright. Let's go," he said with great spirit. "Oh, we have boxed dinners in the kitchen the staff left for us. And I'm starving."

McCager, mouth dropped, was staring in absolute disbelief. Stella smiled.

"Chatty needs a strong hand and lots of attention."

McCager nodded. "Yes, the lots of attention I knew about. Next time, I'll remember the strong hand."

Pepper came out of the kitchen with an armload of boxed food. "C'mon, Chatty. Time to eat, say your prayers, and go to bed."

With nary a complaint, Chatty was up from the sofa and said, "Thank you, Governor, I've had a lovely day with you."

McCager Burnett was still shaking his head in amazement as the DNR vehicle pulled away with Stella, Pepper, and the biggest headache he had ever had.

Chapter Nineteen

CR

The DNR van belonging to the state of Georgia pulled up in front of two cottages sitting about forty feet apart.

One cottage was vintage-pretty with a roomy porch, green shutters that had started to fade, and a door and screen door that matched it. There was a porch swing with cushions and two handbuilt rocking chairs.

The other cottage, though, was ragged and unpainted. Its porch heaved with sadness as though it might fall in at any moment. Each cottage had a meager porch light which were turned on and faintly glowed.

As they drove up, the ranger said, "Maybe next time you come back you can stay at the Sears and Roebuck house over at Mud River. I think Mr. Reynolds might have gotten tired of people coming to visit and stayin' with him at the Big House—so he ordered the house from the Sears and Roebuck catalog. Mighty fine piece of work. I'm guessin' it was from around the mid-1940s. It's a little beauty and built as well or better than anything today. It isn't far off the river. But one of our big shots from Atlanta is in town and he's stayin' over there. Hope this'll do you fair enough."

"I'm sure it will," Stella said as she took Pepper's hand and stepped out of the van. When Chatty saw where they were spending the night, he practically had to be pulled out of the van. Finally, reluctantly, he emerged. The four of them stood in the dark of night, looking at the spare cottages. Stella walked over to the poorest looking of the two then sighed, happily. She tossed a hand toward the run-down house and said, "Now, *THIS is my people*."

Pepper threw back his head and laughed while Chatty sniffed haughtily and said, "Well, good, then that's where you can stay. Pepper and I will stay in the 'adorable cottage'." He made quotes with his fingers around adorable cottage. "I really don't want to spend the night within the same walls as Pepper but it would be inappropriate for you to stay in the house with him and just as inappropriate for you and I to share intimate quarters." He raised his eyebrows as if to say, "You know what I mean."

The laughter from Pepper's gut stopped the minute he realized, or rather remembered, that he had to share a house with Chatty for the night.

"Sir, how many bedrooms does this cute house have?" Pepper asked.

"Three. And two small bathrooms. We rent it out on occasion. That 'un," motioning toward the worn-out little house, "has two bedrooms and one bath. That okay with y'all?"

"Absolutely!" Stella said. They were in the middle of tremendously primitive conditions and she felt right at home.

She could feel the warmth of home wrapping itself around her. Sapelo Island was like the Appalachian foothills for her except that it was surrounded by water where, at home, they had only the river running through their land.

Pepper picked up Stella's small bag and his, saying to Chatty, "I take it you can carry your own bag?"

"Valise," Chatty replied snobbishly.

The DNR ranger said, "I've already unlocked the cottages for y'all. Of course, to be truthful, we don't lock up around here. We all trust each other and abide by the law of the land and the Good Book. That's why all of this is so surprising. It's unsettling. Ms. Bankwell, let me turn some lights on for you." He scurried up the steps then reappeared after a moment.

"Where would y"all like for me to take the boxes of food?" he asked.

Chatty spoke up. "In *that* cottage," he said, pointing to the nicer of the two cottages. "That other one, I feel most assuredly, has termites or mice or moles."

Stella rolled her eyes. "Moles live in the ground."

"I can always count on the mountain girl to know these things."

Pepper shook his head in exasperation. "It seems to me you could do with a little educating on the ways of nature and of common folks."

Chatty, valise in hand, was climbing the steps onto the porch. "No, sir, I'm fine, thank you. I have people who are paid to know those things."

His reply annoyed Pepper but Stella hid her smile behind her hand. Chatty was a handful but, goodness, how she
loved him.

CR

The trio had finished dinner and Chatty had chosen the best
bedroom, the one with a king-sized bed and a bath attached.
Still, he turned up his nose and gave a bit of shudder. Maybe,
he had groaned, he could make it for one night without his
luxury sheets.

Stella worried about that. She knew it was probably a low
thread count and he was used to D. Porthault Fine Linens.
But she told herself, he was the one who insisted on coming.
After dinner and goodnights were said, and Chatty had
thrown his arms around Stella (proclaiming his love for her
and that it was important for her to know should the Good
Lord call him home before daybreak and if God could find
him in such dreary place) Stella had gone to her cottage, perfectly satisfied and happy to hear a screen door squeak and
slam behind her.

"It's stuffy in here," Chatty complained after he had
taken his shower and adorned himself in custom made silk
pajamas. He reminded Pepper of the movie star, William
Powell, in the film series, *The Thin Man.*

"Raise your window," replied the unsympathetic Pepper
as he read a pamphlet about the Island.

"I tried. It's stuck."

Pepper, too, tried to open the window but couldn't. "You're close to the front door. We'll leave the door open and get fresh air through the screen door."

Chatty looked skeptical. "What if someone comes in to and rob us?"

Pepper was getting close to being mad. "You heard the officer say that they leave all the doors unlocked. Here, I'll lock the screen door with this latch. Does that make you happy?"

"Pepper, I will not be happy until I return to the luxury of my home but, yes, it does make me *happier.*"

Stella settled in quite nicely in her rustic abode and all was well until sometime after midnight. Despite his misgivings, Chatty had gone easily to sleep on the cheap sheets and was even snoring when he felt warm air on his ear. It felt good, even lovely. He snuggled deeper in the sheets and blankets, a slight smile on his face. That didn't last long. He felt something like a wet washcloth covering his ears. Then, suddenly, he came awake and immediately turned on the light. There, trying to lick his face, was the cow that had chased Chatty around the Reynolds Mansion. Horror struck and he jumped up, onto the bed, screaming. Pepper, dressed only in boxers without a tee shirt, grabbed his pistol from the nightstand.

In seconds, he was in Chatty's room where he saw the hilarious sight of Chatty, in custom-made yellow and white striped silk pajamas, clinging to a pillow, with a lovelorn cow lowing sweetly to him in a mating call.

"Shoo! Shoo! Do you hear me? Shoo!"

Pepper was bent over with laughter. Every time he tried to stop laughing, he started again. Chatty, needless to say, was far from amused.

"I could use some professionalism here," snapped Chatty as the cow moved closer. "This time, shoot him."

When, at last, Pepper could mildly stop laughing, he replied, "If I shoot that cow, we will be in worse shape than we are now because we can't get him out if he's dead."

Chatty was running from one side of the bed to the other. Wherever he went, the cow went. "Though it does seem to me that, even alive, you're not getting him out of here."

Jackson Culpepper had been raised on the outskirts of Memphis. He was more of suburbanite than a city fella, but he certainly was not a country boy. He knew little about cows, but he was fairly certain that they were harmless. The cow, standing between the bed and wall, resisted Pepper's prodding to leave. Regardless of how much he pushed, the cow stood its ground.

"Call Stella!" Chatty exclaimed. "She's always bragging about being the farm girl. She'll know what to do."

Pepper had to concede that was a good idea so he called Stella's cell phone. "Sorry to wake you but we need some of your farm expertise over here, immediately. Please, don't tarry."

Stella, dressed in navy satin pajama bottoms and a navy cotton tank top, grabbed a matching cotton cardigan, put on her shoes and, with phone in-hand, ran next door where the screen door had been demolished and was now lying on the porch floor. What she found next was so unbelievable that when she could get her breath from laughing, she borrowed Pepper's phone to take a photo of Chatty standing on top of the bed in his satin pajamas, clutching a pillow with Pepper, who had put on his trousers, now pushing the cow.

"Stella Faye, this is no time for making memories," Chatty chastised frantically. "You're a farm girl. How do we get this beast out of here?"

"I've never gotten one out of a bedroom."

"Try!" Chatty snapped.

Stella joined Pepper in trying to push fifteen hundred pounds of wild beef but it wasn't moving.

Pepper gave up and asked, "Is this the same cow from the Reynolds house?"

Stella nodded. "I'm pretty sure it is. I'm certain, though, that I have never seen a cow climb steps, tear down a door, and walk into a house. Why does this feral cow love Chatty so much?"

"Feral? *FERAL?* What is that? Is that something like rabies?" Chatty exclaimed. He was close to panic. No, it's probably fairer to say he *was* panicked.

"Calm down, Chatty. It means he's wild. Not domesticated." She turned to Pepper. "Usually, when an animal is feral, he won't come close to a human. But this one seems smitten with Chatty. I don't understand."

"I don't understand, either," Pepper replied sarcastically, meaning he had no idea how anyone or anything could fall in love with Chatty.

An idea struck Stella from out of the blue. Or heaven. "Chatty, are you wearing cologne?"

"Most certainly."

"I thought you took a shower," Pepper remarked.

"I did and then I put on my cologne."

"To go to bed?" The ways of Chatham Balsam Colquitt IV were beyond understanding for Pepper.

"I am a gentleman, sir. What if I died in the middle of the night? I would certainly want to smell good for the undertaker."

Pepper threw up his hands in retreat.

"I think it's possible there's something in the cologne that's attracting the cow." Stella and her incredible memory was at work again. She was trying to draw on something way back in her memory.

"Yeah, otherwise, why would this cow be interested in Chatty?"

Chatty threw a mean look to Pepper. "Sometime, I will introduce you to Tara Beth McComb. She will answer *that* question."

Stella paid no attention to their childish bickering. "Where is your cologne?"

"Inside my cologne bag, inside my shaving kit, inside my valise. In the bathroom."

Stella went in the bathroom and dug through the layers until she found the bottle. She came out with the opened bottle, sprayed a bit of cologne into the air near the cow and, suddenly, the cow spun around and came toward her.

"Oh, my precious Stellie, don't get killed by that wild beast," Chatty yelled while jumping up and down on the bed but not worried enough to help the friend he adored.

Using the fragrance, Stella continued leading the cow out of the house, down the steps, and about a hundred yards away. Then she ran for the cute little cottage, slamming the door behind her. With a racing heart, she fell against the door.

"You mean to tell me that cow was attracted to Chatty just because of his cologne?" the bare chested, very handsome Pepper asked. (This was the first time that Stella had seen Pepper without a shirt and she had to admit that he was quite fetching.)

"Chatty, do you know if this cologne has sandalwood in it?" Stella asked.

He was still standing atop the bed, clutching the pillow.

"Most certainly. It is the top note. I have it custom made in Paris."

"That's it," Stella replied. "Cows are attracted to the scent of sandalwood. I learned that in 4-H Club—which, by the way, Chatty you once claimed was of no use in life."

Suddenly, Chatty, who had been scared to death, had a crestfallen reaction. "You mean it wasn't me? She didn't love *me*?"

"Five minutes ago, you didn't want her to love you," Stella said.

He dropped the pillow, then fell to his knees on the mattress, a sad look on his face. "I changed my mind."

This was what made Stella always love Chatty, even when he was at his most aggravating and demanding—he was nothing more than a child who wanted to be loved. Stella threw a cautionary look at Pepper not to say anything, then said to Chatty, "As long as I'm alive, you will always be loved." Stella replied, smiling sweetly.

Chatty basked in the moment. The truth being that Chatham Balsam Colquitt IV was the richest man in Atlanta—possibly Georgia—and, yet he was the loneliest, too.

After he had basked for a while, Stella couldn't resist saying, "Just remember: 4-H is important. Without it, you'd still have a cow trying to crawl into bed with you."

CR

Governor McCager Burnett could not eat his eggs for laughing. For most of the day, that laughter hung in his chest and did not threaten to leave anytime soon. The threesome from the two cottages had come over to have breakfast at the Big House as the Gullah Geechees call it. McCager had hired, out of his own pocket, the cooking staff to stay for a couple of days. Two were left but three had already departed since the group was much smaller.

"Governor, it really isn't funny. That wild beast was trying to *kiss me!*"

"Why would any beast want to kiss you?" asked Pepper, in a partially sarcastic, partially serious tone.

Chatty, as amiable as always, replied, "Again, Marshal Culpepper, let me introduce you to Tara Beth McComb. She will happily answer that question.

"Whatever happened to her?" the Governor asked. "She was quite a spirited girl."

Chatty sighed heavily and dropped his chin into his hands. "She met a cowboy from Montana and decided she'd rather be wild and free than chained to the commands of Buckhead society. I get postcards and notes from her every now and then. Her decision to leave, she does not regret one iota." A sadness clouded his face. "Yet another one, gone, that I loved."

The conversation was halted by Sanders who came into the dining room. "I hear y'all would like to take a tour of the Sears Roebuck house over at Mud River?"

Stella and Pepper looked at each other anxiously. They still had three people to interview. The Governor, ever perceptive and always ahead of the game, said, "I've arranged for the three who remained to be interviewed to be brought here from The Oaks. Seems to me that these last three would do well to be interviewed here. I've studied up on them and you've saved the best for last." He looked at his Rolex that his Capitol friends had pitched in to pay for and said, "They won't be here for another hour. You have time. A GBI agent is bringing them over to ensure they don't speak to each other. Y'all go on. Chatty, you're going, too."

"But Governor, I've had such trauma. Yesterday, I almost died as I fell down those deathly stairs. It was horrible. Then the ghastly experience of that cow chasing me, then showing up at my bed in the middle of the night to kiss me."

Something suddenly occurred to Stella. "You aren't wearing that cologne today, are you?"

Most certainly. A gentleman does not leave his house—or shack, in this case—without his fragrance."

"Go to the sink," Pepper demanded as he pointed to enormous steel sink, "and wash it off. Now." Pepper was long past indulging the over-indulged Chatty. "We are not going to deal with that lovesick cow again. We have business to do. Cows have very sensitive noses and will smell you a mile away." There was a pause as Chatty silently resisted. Then, "Go, now." As Chatty dragged, half mad, half disappointed, to the sink, Pepper carried on with business. "Has Joseph gone back to Darien?"

"He has, in fact, but I can get him here on the boat bringing over the witnesses, if you like."

Pepper nodded thoughtfully. "I think he can be useful. He's level-headed and very insightful."

By this time, Chatty, to his great disappointment, had scrubbed off his cologne. "This will be the first time since I was eighteen that I have not worn cologne."

"Sorry that life is so tough for you," the Governor said in a tone that sounded a bit like a warning. "But I have things to do and I am not babysitting as I did yesterday. Now, if Miss Alva were here, she'd pet you and make over you. But I'm not that kind. You are going wherever Stella goes today because, apparently, she is the only one who knows how to manage you."

Chatty did not dare dispute the Governor. Oh, no. He loved the Burnetts and he felt like the Governor was the same kind of father to him as his own, beloved father. There was a sense of continuity that seemed to pass from his father to the Governor and it gave comfort to Chatty.

"Yes, sir."

With a few more bites of toast and sips of coffee, the three finished breakfast and headed for Mud River.

СЯ

The DNR SUV pulled up to a well-maintained house that was one and a half stories and trimmed out in red. They drove up to the side where a red-trimmed screen door welcomed them. Pepper and Stella climbed out of the SUV in awe, silently admiring a well-built house with no house or neighbor anywhere close by. The air was still and the edge of the beautiful Mud River was just forty feet from the house.

"Any trouble with flooding?" Pepper asked. Something that perfect had to have an imperfection.

"None," Sanders responded. "We have to deal with mice, though. Darnedest thing. We can't figure it out. We have cats and traps but still, they keep coming. Fortunately, they don't do any real damage. C'mon, let's take a tour."

Chatty had to remark, "Well, this is the best thing I've seen on this primitive island so far. Other than the Reynolds house, that is. *That house* I understand. My ancestors would have been friends with the Reynolds, I'm quite sure. They knew all the important people in America and many in Europe."

The tour was worth it. The house was set fully-furnished with lovely antiques, books, board games, and photos of the island in the early years.

"I could live happily ever after in this home. A home built from a catalog," Stella commented.

"Me, too," Pepper agreed. "And I'm a Memphis boy."

"Mama told me, that when she was a little girl and lived in a tin-roofed shack, that she used to look at the Sears Roebuck catalog, at these houses, and dream that one day her Daddy could buy one of them." Stella smiled at the remembrance.

Chatty did not like the sound of that, not at all—especially when a knowing, almost loving look passed between Stella and Pepper. "Okay, we can just stop this fairyland talk and move on. We have a murder to solve and the way you two are acting, it's once again going to fall to me to solve it."

Sanders said, "I want to show you the barn." By this time, he had already gotten a good understanding of Chatty and said to him, "I don't think this will be up your alley."

"Well, I saw that old fashioned bowling alley in the basement of the Reynolds house. It was the first time I ever saw a bowling alley. I thought that was an urban legend—that people bowl." A beat. "I've never known anyone who bowls. It's sounds so common."

Pepper was becoming more passive aggressive with Chatty. "Of course, you haven't."

"And, Pepper Culpepper, that means… what?"

"That you're too affected by high society to go bowling." He wanted to say "snobby" but that would have pushed it too far with Stella and Chatty.

Stella stepped in quickly. "Where's the barn?"

"Over here, Ma'am," Sanders replied. "We can walk to it." He then looked down at her flat but fancy sandals and said, "I think you'll be fine to climb the stairs."

Stella now looked down at her shoes, knowing his thoughts. "Sir, I can take these shoes off and go barefoot if I need to. I'm a mountain girl. I'll do what it takes."

Chatty rolled his eyes, "Oh, here we go again with that 'mountain girl' number. She wears it like a badge of honor."

"She wears it to show her authenticity and not to put on airs," Pepper countered. "Besides, it came in handy for you last night."

Chatty just shook his head and walked off toward the barn, still attired in his equestrian outfit that had been cleaned and repaired yesterday by the staff at the Reynolds house. That was the day that McCager Burnett would never forget and make him look differently at those terrible, contentious days in Congress. Sometimes, the most memorable days are aggravating but still entertaining.

CR

The group made their way to the barn and were stunned at what they saw. At least Stella and Pepper were taken aback.

"This reminds me of the ruins of Ephesus," Stella said. She had once taken a cruise around Greece and Italy, in the days when money came easy, and she thought herself in love with the dashingly handsome husband who had ended up betraying her. It was all a fantasy. Stella shook herself out of the memory and returned to the moment at hand.

The barn was mostly made of stone, obviously built before the Civil War. Sanders said, "Let me show you somethin' special." They climbed the steps, some easier than others. Chatty, with a few too many pounds, struggled a bit but refused to admit it. They reached the second floor.

"This is where the hay was kept. They threw it down for the cows, using pitch forks," said Sanders, showing a big opening on one side of the barn.

"They didn't feed that beast that broke into our house and tried to kill me, did they?"

Sanders looked quizzical at Chatty. Then Pepper explained, "One of the feral cows has taken a loving to Chatty because he wears an expensive cologne."

"Did it have sandalwood in it?" Sanders asked. "It's the top note in the scent," Chatty replied proudly, never considering that a rugged DNR officer might have no clue as to what Chatty was talking about. Of course, he had to add, "It's custom designed in Paris."

The officer chuckled. "First of all, the cows were brought here to the island as domesticated cows. Over the last several decades or so, they've become feral and just forage for food. No amount of interaction with people will make a feral a domestic. They have a highly developed sense of smell and sandalwood, particularly, attracts them."

"Yeah, Chatty was devastated when he discovered it was his cologne and not himself." Pepper couldn't resist.

Everyone laughed and Chatty sulked. "I wasn't devastated, that isn't true. I was, at best, let down."

Stella walked over to the front side of the barn, to a large opening where she could stand up and look out, over the unspoiled nature of Sapelo Island. There were no house developments or shopping centers. "Oh, to live in a place like this," she said longingly.

"Yeah, but if you get sick in the middle of the night, what then? There's not even a nurse around." Pepper remarked.

"If I'm sick enough, I'll die in Paradise." Then, something caught Stella's eye. "What're those?" She pointed to square holes scattered across the wall, beside where she was standing.

"Carrier pigeon holes," he replied. "For years, that was how the island got messages from the mainland. Pigeons flew in messages, dropped them, got a bit of food and water, then headed back to the mainland."

Chatty wondered aloud, "Carrier pigeons? I thought they were a fable that somebody made up. Or a parable from the Bible."

Stella rolled her eyes. Chatty and his interpretation of the Bible, all from the little he heard while overseeing church bingo on Thursday nights and occasional Sunday mornings.

Pepper walked over and inspected the holes. "That's amazing. I studied this at Glynco when I was preparing to become a Marshal. You know, I think pigeons are still used in some places. Maybe San Quentin."

For fifteen or so minutes, they carefully studied and talked about the ancient forty or so holes.

"Are these still being used?" Stella asked.

"Oh, no," Sanders replied. "These haven't been used in years."

While everyone else wandered back to the steps, leaving Stella alone, Sanders looked over and reminded her, "Be careful of the floor. It's old and you might fall through at any place—though you're pretty small and shouldn't have any problem."

Stella stayed for several more minutes, completely intrigued. She thought about what must go into training pigeons and what it must take to teach them their destination. But, like the telegraph and shorthand, they had fallen by the wayside. Still, it was astounding that Sapelo Island, with only some 300 or so people, had faster Internet than on St. Simons Island and even stronger cell service. She shrugged. Oh well, maybe the pigeons were without work for a reason. And perhaps they liked retirement.

Maybe, she thought, smiling, there's a pension for the pigeons. Somewhere they go to retire to have medical care and plenty of food and water. Like the ducks at the Peabody Hotel in Memphis where they change ducks every thirty days after which they went to even greater happiness somewhere else to be well-cared-for. She was just too much of an animal lover because her heart was tender and sometimes it hurt too much when animals suffered. Stella turned around and headed for the steps.

But as she started down, she looked back where something caught her attention.

Chapter Twenty

❧

McCager had decided to sit in on the last interviews. This, Stella knew and did not mind at all. In fact, that was why he had arranged to have the remaining witnesses brought over. Sheriff Goudelock was tied up in court for the morning but would have them there by eleven. He, of course, had already interviewed everyone so he saw no reason to be there. He had a mountain of paperwork to do as well as court. Murder or not, it still caused a mountain of paperwork.

Chatty, caring not at all about the interviews, announced he would be taking a nap in one of the rooms upstairs at the Big House. "Yesterday was the most traumatizing day of my life. I was almost called to my heavenly home—and I would like to put that off for as long as possible. I fear it will be a step down from my current lifestyle. And that cow? Breathing in my ear, then trying to kiss me, was horrible." He shuddered and closed his eyes, tightly. "It was all too much." He looked upward and asked, "Lord, what have I done so wrong to deserve such torment?"

"Oh, stop it, Chatty," Stella said firmly. "First of all, cows don't kiss. And, secondly, come help me in the church food pantry some Saturday and you'll see real misery. Now, go take a couple of aspirins and lie down," she smiled. "We'll all feel better if you do."

"Stella Faye, you need to love on me more than you do. When I'm feeling neglected by my favorite girl, I act out."

Again, it was times such as this that both melted her heart and made her laugh. Chatty was always so transparent. She walked over, hugged him, kissed his cheek, then asked, "Should I come up and tuck you in and say prayers with you?"

He shook his head and said, as he walked away, "Oh, Stellie, sometimes you take things too far. It's just a nap."

ᗇ

The four of them had a discussion as to which person to call in first. It really came down to interviewing Ance McCoy, first or last, because he would be the key person. Finally, as Stella, smarter than most people ever expected, pointed out that if he gave them any new information, one of them could be tracking it down while the others were interviewed.

Joseph had come over on the boat with the remaining witnesses. He had decided to walk the yard and look over the rest of the house, despite Chatty warning him, "There are wild beasts out there. You be careful. One might try to kiss you."

For Joseph, raised up in Sparta, where on occasion you might find a homeless person staggering around with a cheap bottle of wine in one hand and a cigarette in the other, this was laughable. But he didn't make that comment because he realized he was on a primitive island and could encounter an alligator or something serious. Of course, he had brought along his handgun, tucked in the back of his pants, just in case.

The group settled comfortably in the living room and Ance was brought in by a Deputy. They then pointed to a cozy chair and asked if Ance would like some water. He nodded. "Very much."

He cracked the top of the bottle, took a sip, then signaled, "I'm ready to go."

"Mr. McCoy, we appreciate your time and understand you've had to stay two days longer here than you planned," Pepper started.

"I'm good. I want to help find whoever killed my best friend. Of course, what I'd like most is to find out it was an accident." He took another sip of a water. He was an average-sized man, with a bit of a paunch, thin, graying hair and a face that was completely pleasant, accentuated by sweet, blue eyes. "It's hard to imagine anyone would want to kill Spence. He was always kind and tremendously generous. Once, we had a salesperson in our office whose son had just been diagnosed with cancer. Spencer paid everything the insurance didn't. That's the sort of man he was."

"No enemies you know of?"

He thought for a long bit. "No. He had, recently, broken up with a woman who seemed very angry and who was coming after him all the time."

"In what ways?" Stella asked.

"Constantly calling and texting. You know. Spencer had to get a new phone number which, as you can imagine, was a big deal for him. He'd had the same number for twenty years. But then, she would come by the office and make a scene or at his house. He had a gated entrance, but she knew the code 'cuz he hadn't changed it. He finally hired some private security. They didn't come here to the island since everyone thought he'd be safe. And we'd kept it secret—where we were going."

"We know she lived in Nashville. How often did she come to Greenwood?" McCager asked.

"Fairly regularly." He chuckled. "They all knew her by name at the Alluvian Hotel. In fact, about six months ago, thinking Spencer was going to marry her, she bought a condo around the corner from the Alluvian. Not a good move. That really made Spencer feel cornered. And he was still in love with his first wife. No question. I've spoken to her and she's beyond devastated. She was a good person, just not in love with Spencer. But, oh, how she tried to be. She knew how wonderful he was and how much he loved her."

Stella nodded, "Yes, we've heard that. Let me ask, did anything happen that night that seemed odd—or out of place?"

Ance sat, thinking, a few moments. "The only thing I can recall was that we had a different chef that night than we'd had the first three nights. He was brought in and introduced as one of Europe's finest. The other chef, we were told, had a family emergency and needed to leave."

"Any arguments you recall?"

"A couple of firings happened but they were sad not mad. Spencer was so hurt that he had to do it he started drinking Jack Daniel's Black Label after the firings. He wasn't much of a drinker, but he poured it on that night. He was drunk. I hate to say it but he was. That's the first thing I thought of when I found him laying in—" Here, he stopped to gather himself. Having seen his best friend like that, he would never forget it. "When I saw him at the foot of the steps, I thought he had stumbled down because he was so drunk." Tears welled in Ance's eyes. "I shouldn't have gone to bed and left him. Then, this wouldn't have happened."

"Could you tell us about the last time you saw him?" Stella wondered.

Ance McCoy's eyes saddened. "We went into the kitchen to get a bite to eat. Only he, Kyle Kirby, and I were still up. Twelve had left on the last ferry that afternoon. Kyle and Mrs. Martin had stayed so he could dismiss them. Anyway, we went in the kitchen and found a couple of staff who were still on duty, including the new chef. We sat at the table eating cheese, crackers and prosciutto, things like that, when Spence asked the chef for a peanut and jelly sandwich. I remember thinking, 'Most who were raised like him would ask for caviar.'"

"How did y'all part?" Pepper asked.

"Kirby left first. He said goodnight, even shook hands with Spencer and told him, 'It's been a pleasure.' After he left, Spence told me that he had given Kirby enough severance to see him through to sixty-two where he could then take retirement or continue to live off of savings. Kirby was careful with money except that his wife had recently talked him into buying a ridiculously expensive house. We used to joke that Kirby had the first nickel he ever made. I think it hurt, at first, but then Kirby saw the good in it all—more time to spend with his wife and a grandbaby coming soon. I consoled Spence for a while but pretty soon he'd had so much Jack Daniel's in him that he wasn't hearing me. So, I took a last sip of wine, I didn't even finish the glass, and I left. I don't recall seeing any staff at all."

Ance, once again, sat there, thinking. "I went up to my room—which was right over the kitchen. This house is so old that you can hear the water running through the kitchen pipes. And I heard some kind of clatter. I wasn't sure what it was. Like a big thump. I ignored it, then tried to sleep, but couldn't. Finally, a while later, I realized I didn't have any water and I needed to take some medication. So, I went back, down to the kitchen, to get ginger ale to both settle my stomach and take the medicine. All the lights were out except for one. That's when I discovered Spencer at the foot of the basement stairs."

"What led you down there?" Pepper asked.

"The door was open and the light was on. The staircase light. I saw Mrs. Graham. She was dressed for bed.

233

Apparently, she was headed over to close the door. I got to the door just as she did, coming from the other side. I went over to turn off the light and that's when I glanced down and saw his body lying there." True sorrow covered him and he grew misty-eyed. "I think I'm still in shock. It'll be a nightmare I'll always live with."

They all felt sorry for him, even McCager. You could see it in his own eyes. After a moment, Pepper finished by saying, "Thank you, Mr. McCoy. We've read the interview that you had with Sheriff Goudelock so I think we have everything we need. Do you plan on staying another night?"

"I can stay if it might help."

Stella spoke up. "Mr. McCoy, I think it would help if you stayed, in case we have more questions. You knew Mr. Houghton better than anyone." Stella didn't say anything more, but she'd been thinking that McCoy possibly had something to do with the murder. After all, he'd discovered the body when he wasn't expecting to see Mrs. Graham."

"I'll be happy to stay. Would it be possible for me to go for a walk, to get some fresh air? This is the third day we've been kept in our rooms and I'm starting to feel a little cooped-up."

McCager said, "We're using a room upstairs for officers to watch the other guests but since we have one posted in the front yard, why don't you walk out there and stay in sight so he can see you? I'll let him know it's okay. And since we've gathered your cell phone and computer, there's really no harm."

"Thank you, Governor," Ance nodded as he rose from his chair, shaking hands first with McCager, then Pepper, and smiling at Stella. "Please, let me know if there's anything I can do."

Ance walked across the room and as he started out, he turned around, standing there for a moment, thinking. Then, "This just occurred to me. It may mean nothing at all. In fact, I'm sure it doesn't. But I'll mention it, anyway."

"Please, come back then," McCager suggested.

Ance McCoy walked back to the chair where he had been sitting but remained now on his feet. "I grew up in an unhappy home. That's the only way to describe it. My mother was unkind. She beat on us kids and my parents always seemed to be in a fight. My sister, Tammy, holds a lot of resentment—which is an understatement. Awhile back, she started tracing our family history. You know, looking into our family tree. I'm not sure how all that works but somehow she discovered that our great-Grandfather had become addicted to a tonic he took for all the aches and pains a farmer can have. He got addicted to it because it had opium, and cocaine, in it. This was back when that was still legal, before 1914 or so. I don't know how she found out, but that tonic was made by the Malachi Company. In fact, it was the same tonic that started their empire." Ance paused, only momentarily. She has been so angry—calling me, telling me that if I were true to the family, I'd leave the company."

Stella then spoke up. "I think I've lost a step somewhere. Why did his addiction, so far back, matter to her?"

235

"A generational curse, she claims," said McCoy. "You see, we know our Grandfather was beaten by his father, the one with the addiction, then he beat our Mama and Tammy believes that's what made our Mama so mean. Out of my siblings, Tammy got the brunt of our mother's anger so she's always been surly and angry. About two weeks ago, she'd come to my house and said to me, 'I feel like killing that rat you work for, the one you think is such a good friend.' There was such a darkness about her. It was chilling. She started screaming and running around the room. She even picked up a vase and threw it. Again, this may not be anything.... and I don't know how she would even get to the island... but I thought I should mention that I told her a couple of weeks earlier that we were coming to Sapelo. I told her, not thinking it would be a big deal because this was before I saw her anger toward the Houghtons."

McCager, standing up, said, "Mr. McCoy, I think you've given us some very good information. Thank you."

A few minutes after Ance left, he returned. They were surprised to see him. His head dropped, he stood there for a minute before, finally, the Governor asked, "Is there anything else?"

Ance nodded quietly. He struggled to find the words and get started. "I left something out that is important, I guess. I didn't mention it because I thought I'd become a suspect but I would never harm Spencer. He meant so much to me." He paused and the room waited. "That night, after he had so

236

much whiskey and I had had a bit, it hit me hard, we got into a loud argument in the kitchen."

"Over what?" asked Stella.

"We are under a federal audit." He sighed as a tear rolled down his cheek. "Kyle Kirby had made several mistakes in our returns. I'm responsible for checking but I hadn't. It raised red flags and now it's grown pretty serious. Kyle didn't make them on purpose. He was in over his head. That's why, when Spencer fired him, that he didn't make that an issue. He knew it was just incompetence. It was the first argument we've ever had and I blame it on the whiskey. He was angry because of the stress of the audit and his former girlfriend were driving him crazy. The board wanted him to fire me but he refused. That was added pressure. I am so miserably sad that my last words with him were angry. He was blaming me for everything. And, really, I am to blame. I should have just taken his anger because I deserved it."

Pepper spoke. "Well, this does change things and now makes you our top suspect. We'll need to keep an officer with you constantly."

Ance nodded. "I understand." Pepper stood, intending to find a GBI agent who could guard Ance but, before he left, Ance spoke again. "I understand why you would suspect me but I still believe that you should check on my sister, Tammy. She is wild with anger toward Spencer."

After Ance McCoy, escorted by an agent, left the room, the Governor sat back down and he, Stella, and Pepper discussed the new development and how Tammy might've hired a private boat, or come by the ferry under another name, to the island. In fact, they got so caught up in what Ance had told them that they had forgotten to bring down the other two witnesses who were still waiting, Nate McCullough and Denizen Walker.

Stella had an idea. "I have a good friend in Greenville. Let me give her a call and see if I can find out anything else." That call, of course, would produce a surprise for them all.

Chapter Twenty-One

CR

Stella dialed Julia Belle Benson's number and, just when she thought her call was going into voicemail, Julia Belle answered. The two women had gone to college together and stayed in touch ever since.

"Hello, friend!" Julia Belle said gayly. "It's been months since I've talked to you. How is everything?"

Stella explained why she was reaching out to Julia Belle, finishing by saying, "So, in short, I'm trying to find out more about Ance."

"Well, Ance McCoy is a legend in Greenville, a town filled with legends. He came from the poor side of town and worked himself into a millionaire. He earned it but, as I've heard, his best friend was a scion of the family who owns the company—I'm guessing he's the one who died?"

"That's right. Ance has a sister named Tammy. Do you know her?"

"Tammy Mumford? Oh, yes. She's the biggest nut in town. She has absolutely no social graces and is not at all beloved, that's for sure. But I don't know what more I can tell you."

"Can you try to find out anything else?"

"Absolutely. Give me one hour. I am in the garden club with her next-door neighbor. I'll call her. Then, I'll call Maxine at the beauty shop where she goes. I'll get the complete lowdown. Keep that phone close by. You do have service on Sapelo, don't you?"

"Perfect service."

"Great. Talk to you soon."

While they waited for Julia Belle to call back, they had lunch and discussed the case.

"Ance is our first real suspect but now Tammy Mumford has become a viable suspect," McCager said. "She wanted to kill Spencer Houghton and knew he was on the island."

Joseph had joined them for lunch and pointed out, "I went around the house but didn't see any broken limbs on bushes next to windows, or footsteps in places they shouldn't be. I checked with the gardener, too. He hasn't cut the grass or trimmed the bushes since the day before Mr. Houghton died. The entire landscaping crew had been busy planting trees down the road. But the gardener brought up again the fight he saw between Mr. Houghton and Campbell Puckett."

Stella turned to Joseph. "I can't buy into that. Every person talks about how kind Spencer Houghton was and the same goes for Campbell. I believe what Campbell says, that it was just an animated discussion. I have those all the time. If someone saw me and Chatty from afar, they'd think we were in an argument. So, is there any chance that this could be an accident?"

Joseph, having just taken a bite of chicken, shook his head, firmly. He finished chewing and swallowed. "No ma'am. I absolutely believe that he was killed." Again, he explained his theory of how he had been pushed down the stairs and into the high concrete beam which then caused the head injury and neck break when he fell so hard, probably hitting the wall, and bouncing back to where he was found.

Chatty, well-rested from his nap, was now adding his two cents. "Look at how I fell. I proved, right there, that you could survive without deadly injuries." He dabbed at the corner of his mouth with his napkin. "Of course, I wasn't drunk."

Pepper narrowed his eyes at Chatty. "And I did throw myself across the stairs to soften your landing. I have the bruises and sore leg to prove it."

"Oh, Pepper, let's not take my glory. I did the real work. I tumbled from the top to the bottom," Chatty retorted, comically. "And in so doing, made a very big difference in this case."

As Pepper started to reply, Stella's little flip phone dinged. "That has to be Julia Belle. Excuse me," she said, jumping up from the table.

"Girlfriend, have I got the scoop for you," Julia Belle began.

"I can't wait to hear."

"I called Kim Watson, who lives next door to Tammy. She said she's always been a kook but that lately she'd gotten very angry. About a month ago, Kim was trimming back her

241

rose bushes when Tammy came outside complaining about how her husband always tracked mud in the house. Then, all of a sudden, the conversation turned. Tammy told her she had been doing her family tree and discovered that all their family problems started with some kind of tonic that the Malachi company made. She said, 'It makes me so mad that I could kill every one of them. They ruined an entire family.'"

"Oh, my," said Stella. "That sounds serious."

"Well, that's not all. Maxine at the beauty shop does Tammy's hair. It's a little too brassy blonde for my taste but I like Maxine. She probably just does what Tammy wants. Anyway, back to the real headline: the news on TV that day was all about a shooting in Chicago where three people were killed. And that's when Tammy starts talking about wanting to kill the Houghton family, yelling, 'And my brother works for the SOB and takes their contaminated money! They've ruined our family for four generations!' From what I found out, I sure wouldn't want to be in a room alone with her."

"Julia Belle, you should be a detective!" Stella exclaimed.

"All you need to remember is to call the beauty shop. Whatever you need to know, they know."

"I owe you, my friend. Let's meet in Memphis soon and have a spa weekend at the Peabody."

"Deal."

Stella went back to the dining room and reported what she'd been told.

McCager said, "I'm calling the Sheriff to arrange a look at the ferry passenger list the day before as well as the day of

242

and the day after the murder. While I do that, have Ance brought inside. Let's get a description of his sister and find out just exactly where she might be."

∞

Ance McCoy asked for a cup of coffee, then lifted the cup to his lips with trembling hands. "I can't believe this. I can't believe my own sister would kill anyone, especially my best friend for most of my adult life."

"You're still a suspect," Cager reminded him sternly in that Governor-way of his.

"You said that she knew about this retreat and where y'all would be?" Pepper asked.

He nodded "yes." "We talked last week and I told her that my wife would be in Memphis while I was on Sapelo. She asked about who was going and whether this was a reward trip or company meeting. That's when my sister got so upset and started screaming, eventually storming out of my house."

Stella spoke up now, "Ance, I'm so sorry. I know this is painful. You've lost your best friend and now you're a suspect and it looks like your sister could possibly be responsible if you didn't do it. We need a description of her so we can check with the ferry staff and review the passenger list."

"Uh, yeah, if I had my phone, I could show you a photo but I think it's still locked in the safe at The Oaks. She's about 5'6", has bright blonde hair, maybe thirty pounds overweight. She used to be the prettiest girl you could imagine but, like our mother, anger has stolen her looks."

"Ance, we appreciate your cooperation. Go back to your room and rest. I'm sorry but we have to keep an officer posted outside your door. We'll see if we can get your phone but while we're waiting, we'll go to the dock and ask around," Stella said.

"Shall I come?" Chatty asked.

"No." Pepper didn't even think about it.

"But I'm so much help."

"You're usually more trouble than you are help," Pepper replied, dryly.

"Alright, boys, let's not fight," Stella said, soothingly. "Chatty, you can come but stay out of trouble."

Pepper shot Stella a look of annoyance while Chatty smoothed the lapels on his equestrian suit and jumped up from the table, mindful to push in his chair.

ʘ

Not surprisingly, there was no Tammy Mumford on the ferry's passenger list. A description was useless because there was nothing that made her stand out in the crowd since so many who boarded the ferry wore hats and sunglasses.

"We'll run through the video again but she sounds pretty ordinary looking," said Joe Ray, who was supervisor over the ferry schedule and passengers.

"Thank you, Joe Ray. If you think of anything at all, call the Big House."

Chatty had been very good and well-behaved. "If I had a lollipop, I'd give you one," Pepper mumbled.

As they climbed into the truck, Chatty said, "Really, Pepper, if I didn't know better, I'd think you don't like me. But I know better. Everybody likes me, even you." He threw back his wonderful mane of thick hair and laughed joyfully.

By the time they arrived back at the Reynolds House, Joe Ray had left a message for Stella to call him.

"Don't feel bad, Pepper," Chatty said. "He asked for her because she's so beautiful."

Pepper grinned. "You're right. I would ask for her, too."

"Joe Ray, this is Stella Bankwell." She stopped and listened, making a puzzled face while he talked. "I don't know what that means. Well, thank you for calling. We'll look into it." Stella hung up the phone and turned to the others.

"What do we need to look into?" Chatty asked, anxiously, while Pepper glared at him mildly.

Stella, still puzzled by what Joe Ray had told her, just shook her head. "I don't know what to say."

About that time, McCager walked in, slamming the door behind him. "You won't believe what I just heard."

Chapter Twenty-Two

❧

The group looked from one to another until Chatty said, "Stellie knows something Joe Ray said but she hasn't told us yet."

Cager looked at her. "Oh? Then, you go first."

"Joe Ray said that on the day Mr. Houghton died—well, he thinks it was that day but couldn't swear by it—a woman got off the ferry. She was tall, with broad shoulders, and had on a large, straw hat and sunglasses. She was dressed in jeans and a flowing top. She was also carrying a shoulder bag. At first glance, he thought it was a man, despite the way she was dressed. But then she tripped on the gangplank and dropped a magazine. Joe Ray picked up the magazine and, handing it back to the woman, or to the man, this person said, 'Thank you.' The reason it stuck out in his mind is that it sounded like a man trying to sound like a woman."

The Governor absorbed what Stella said then, finally, said, "That rather bears out to what I just heard. The GBI reported that a state trooper pulled over a speeding car, about thirty miles from here, on I-95. This was sometime yesterday. The trooper then discovered several guns in the car's trunk with the serial numbers filed off—enough to haul in the driver. And when they ran his driver's license, they finally discovered that he's Big Dog Amato."

He paused and looked around the group.

"Big Dog Amato," Pepper repeated, "How do I know that name?"

""From the news!" Stella exclaimed. "Isn't he a hit man with the mob?"

Pepper laughed. "Beautiful, you buzzed in first and outdid me again."

"The only Italians I know are famous designers like the Versaces and Valentino," Chatty added needlessly.

The Governor just closed his eyes and shook his head. These outbursts were one of the annoying but loveable things about Chatty.

"Amato's the one who ratted out everyone for a reduced prison sentence," Pepper said. "He was key to destroying the mob family he was in—then, while he was in the pen, most of the other families went down. When he came out of prison, there was no 'family' to work for. Of course, there were none who would've taken him, anyway. He's been free about three years now and we think he's been working as a freelance contract killer. Everyone's been trying to find him."

Chatty processed this for a moment then announced, "But nothin' about this looks like a mob hit... does it?"

"No, actually, they're very specific about their hits."

With Pepper's confirmation over Chatty's speculation, Chatty sat up and smiled.

Joseph, eating a piece of homemade coconut cake, suggested, "Maybe he had an opportunity to kill in an easy way, so he took it."

The group turned to look at the young man, the one who had started the whole investigation, as he took another bite of cake.

"Terrific thinking," said the Governor, smiling at the young man. "I think you're going to be one of Georgia's great law officers so don't you let another state steal you away."

"It does make sense, though. A man dressed as a woman. Does Amato's size even fit Joe Ray's description?"

Cager was looking down at a note. I don't know what Joe Ray said but Big Dog Amato is 6'2", broad shouldered, two-hundred and twenty pounds."

"Tall and broad shoulders could fit what Joe Ray said," Stella chimed in.

Chatty, who had sashayed off to the kitchen for a piece of the cake he saw Joseph eating, came walking out with a plate and fork. "Do you know that Jolene, in the kitchen, just told me that the chef took off with no warning? Just grabbed his coat and left. No notice. No goodbye. Now, Jolene is left all to herself to cook dinner. Can you believe how rude and inconsiderate people can be?"

Stella, Pepper, and the Governor looked at one another, each sharing the same thought without saying a word while Chatty dug into his cake.

Chapter Twenty-Three

❦

"If he was pretending to be the chef, why would he have stuck around and not left right away?" Stella asked.

"Another hit?" Pepper suggested.

"Or, most probably, to make things seem normal. Remember, until this smart young man," the Governor said, pointing to Joseph, "insisted this wasn't an accident, everyone thought it *was* an accident. Let's talk to Ance again."

The officer brought Ance down and the Governor said to him, "We have a question. Would your sister have enough money to hire a hit man?"

Ance couldn't help but laugh. "I don't know how much a hit man costs but if it's more than a Happy Meal at McDonald's, no. I have to bail her out three or four times a year. She works part-time in the local high school, in the front office, and her husband works as an electrician's assistant."

The Governor sighed, "Thank you, Ance, you can go back to your fine accommodations," and winked at him. The Governor's gut feeling was that Ance was innocent. They all then sat back down at the table and, once again, went over everything they knew, always bumping up against the question: Who would've wanted to kill Spencer Houghton? He was one of the most well-liked, decent people they'd heard of.

And then, suddenly, Stella's photographic memory kicked in. The flash that went through her mind felt like an electrical shock.

She turned to Pepper. "Do you remember your way around the island well enough to get us back to the Mud River house?"

"I think so."

"Grab the keys to the truck that Sanders left."

Before Chatty could get the words out of his mouth—though his mouth was open—Pepper looked at him and said, "No, you can't come this time."

And with that, Stella and Pepper were out the door.

CR

As they bounced along the bumpy, sandy road, Pepper questioned Stella. "What is it? Why are we going there?"

"Pepper, I don't know—except there's something I have to look for."

The road leading to the old Sears and Roebuck house was rough and Stella remarked, "This truck needs a new suspension."

Pepper looked at her, surprised. "What do you know about suspensions?"

"I used to work in racing, remember?"

"Oh, yeah. I keep thinking of you as a debutante." He grinned as she gave him a sideways glance and frowned. As they came in sight of the house, she said, "Stop at the barn. Here!"

Stella then jumped out of the truck and ran to the barn and up the rotting stairs. There, near the pigeonholes, was a piece of paper. She ran over and scooped it up.

"Well done. T," she read out loud.

"Stella, what're you doing?" Pepper asked as he now reached to the top of the steps.

"You know I have a photographic memory. My mind takes snapshots, then files them away in the back of my mind. When we were here earlier, I saw this piece of paper but didn't think much of it." She then turned to Pepper and his handsome face nearly took her breath away—though she forced herself to focus. "I believe someone trained a pigeon that brought this note. If we can decipher it, we'll know who hired Big Dog Amato to kill Houghton."

He shook his head. "Oh, Stella, beautiful Stella, that is a very big jump."

"You just wait, Jackson Culpepper. This note holds the key."

At that moment, they were startled by a voice and turned. "You got here before I did. That note is for me. Hands up, Marshal."

They both were suddenly looking down the barrel of a hunting rifle and decided to do exactly as asked.

Chapter Twenty-Four

CR

Pepper had no idea who was holding a gun on him, but it took Stella only a moment because she had glanced at him as she was headed inside the Reynolds house, earlier that morning.

"You're the gardener, aren't you?" Stella asked.

He nodded. "Most people don't notice the gardener. It's a good cover job to have."

Stella quickly ran it through her mind, then said," A gardener would have an interest in nature. You're the one who trained the pigeon to bring notes here."

He laughed, and rubbed his full, black beard. He was possibly Latin, but it was hard to tell since he had on a billed hat and wore sunglasses. "You're smart. No one thinks carrier pigeons can still be trained. It does take a while, but it can be done."

The gardener then grabbed the note from Stella's hand and smiled with satisfaction. "Sweet Thea," he said softly.

The mumbled name meant nothing to Pepper, but Stella recognized it immediately from their interviews with the assistants: Thea Theressa Olivia Mansford, Thea for short, Spencer's jilted girlfriend—the one who was in such a rage over him breaking up with her. She had hired Big Dog Amato to kill Spencer. But who was this guy, the gardener?

"Two more bodies won't be hard to get rid of." He glanced at the large unglassed window, opposite where they were now standing at gunpoint. "I can push you out that way then use my truck to drag you to the river where there are an awful lot of wild hogs. They'll eat anything."

Stella spoke while trying not to let the fear show in the sound of her voice. "We know that note is from Thea Theressa Oliva Mansford who hired Amato to murder Spencer because she was enraged over their break-up." Pepper's head spun around and he stared at Stella. She had surprised him, again.

"But before you kill us," Stella went on, "at least, tell us who *you* are."

"I'm Jorge. And I've always loved Thea. Now, she realizes it. I've killed for her. I've been on this island for three months since I learned the retreat would be held here. I took this job and I trained the pigeon to bring messages."

"Who sends the messages from the mainland?" Pepper asked.

Jorge shrugged. "Someone who does not have a visa so he will do anything for large amounts of money. It matters not who he is."

Jorge lifted the rifle to his shoulder and focused on Pepper who knew that trying to draw his gun was useless. But just before Jorge pulled the trigger, they heard a vehicle hopping and popping along the bumpy road. With his gun still pointed at them, but now resting closer to his waist, he hurried over to the large open window, near the pigeonholes, to see who it was.

Joseph and Chatty, in the Kubota.

He was so stunned that, for one brief second, he let the rifle's muzzle drift downward and Pepper, always quick to act, wasted no time. Taking three, hurried steps toward Jorge, he pushed him out the window where he fell to the ground, stunned, but still very much alive at Chatty's feet where the rifle landed several inches from Jorge's hand. Chatty jumped higher than he knew was possible for him to jump and Pepper called down, "Grab the gun."

Chatty, rising to the occasion once again, locked onto the rifle and awkwardly trained it on Jorge who rolled over, holding his side, moaning, while Joseph pulled the handgun he'd brought and provided extra coverage. Pepper hurriedly ran down the steps and reached Jorge as he was trying to sit up, Stella close behind Pepper. Chatty was elated, dancing around, as he now sang, "I did it again! I did it again! I'm a hero. I saved the day."

"Yes, Chatty, you did," Stella said, smiling, then planted a big kiss on his face. She winked at Joseph to let him know that he was included.

Pepper, for once, couldn't be annoyed with Chatty. He could only be grateful.

Chapter Twenty-Five

CR

Three days later, the Burnetts threw a big dinner party to celebrate the charges being dropped and Campbell Puckett being freed and cleared. Stella watched members of the Puckett family file in the door of the Governor and Miss Alva's stately Sea Island home and, as she watched, she commented to Pepper, "I don't believe I've ever seen more joy."

Campbell, even nicer and more handsome than Stella had imagined, could not stop smiling while he held tightly to the hand of his girlfriend, Kayla. Like Campbell, she was tall, lean, blonde, and beautiful. They had been dating since their sophomore year in high school and the danger of this event had brought them closer. "I've taken so much for granted in life," He had said. "Never again."

Miss Alva, thoughtful as always, had the dinner catered so that Mrs. Puckett could enjoy it with the family and not do any work. In fact, she hired two extra women to help with the serving and clean-up. Since she and Chatty had identical sets of china, she borrowed extra dishes and made things very special for everyone. Edward Armstrong did the flowers, including a huge arrangement in the front hall, pots of hot-pink geraniums on the porch, and low-setting bouquets for the tables—in addition to the huge dining table, they also used five card tables that were covered in white cloths—and Edward even decorated the mailbox with hydrangeas and bows. The previous day, Mrs. Puckett had polished silver so that it was as beautiful as a formal dinner at the Governor's mansion. China. Silver. Fresh flowers. Crystal. And Chatham Balsam Colquitt IV holding court where he endlessly described, to every guest, his bravery and how, once again, he had saved his sweet Stella. "And, of course, Pepper, too," he would add.

Pepper had had enough of Chatty taking all the credit and opened his mouth at one point but Stella, standing beside him, reached down to take his hand and smiled at him sweetly. For Stella Bankwell, Pepper would do anything—even allow the annoying Chatty to claim all the credit. She looked more beautiful to him than ever that night, wearing a robin's egg-blue, form-fitting dress with a flounce attached (which made her feel young whenever she sashayed across the floor and the ruffle danced). Pepper, in a deep-blue sports jacket, blue shirt, and navy slacks, was a perfect match. A handsome couple... if they were a couple. No one, not even they, themselves, knew whether or not they were a couple. But it didn't matter. Not tonight, anyway. They were just enjoying each other.

At one point, Stella did speak up—because she knew when and how to maneuver Chatty—to save the honor of others. "As for myself, I did nothing. I was scared to death. But with Marshal Culpepper, then Chatty and Joseph driving up at the very second that trigger was about to be pulled, that was all a Godsend. It was all truly miraculous."

At the big dining table where sat the Burnetts, guest of honor Campbell Puckett, Stella, Pepper, Chatty, the Goudelocks, Joseph, Jordan, Campbell's parents, and their dear Mrs. Puckett and her husband, they put together pieces of the mystery that others had missed.

"One thing I've learned is not to get distracted by just one suspect," Stella said. "We should have paid more attention to Thea Theressa Olivia Mansford. If for nothing else, just for having a name like that!" Everyone laughed.

The Governor nodded solemnly then said, "Yes, but I believe with every fiber in my body that Tammy was dangerously close to killing Mr. Houghton. And how sad that would have been for Ance, to have his sister kill his best friend."

"I'm still confused about… is his name Big Dog Amato?" said Miss Alva. "He was really the one hired to kill Mr. Houghton?"

"Exactly," Pepper said. "He called the Reynolds house and left a message that the chef's wife had been in an accident. That's why the chef left so abruptly. Big Dog knew he had to keep his identity from the cameras at the ferry landing so he dressed as a woman. But he arrived in the kitchen as a man to take the other chef's place. He knew there are no cameras at the Reynolds House. And, he managed to slip by being interviewed because he arrived the afternoon of the murder so none of the staff thought about it. They were all strangers to each other. Then, when we started closing in, he bolted and got out there."

"Jorge had long been in love with Thea. He was her gardener and knew she would never settle for him unless he could do something heroic—and for some terribly distorted reason, Jorge thought that killing the man she loved was doing just that. He believed that would make her love him. He didn't know she'd already hired someone to kill Spencer Houghton."

"The things we do for love," sang Chatty.

It was Big Dog, who really should be renamed to Big Squealer who, in order to get himself out of trouble, told them that Jorge had pushed Spencer Houghton down the stairs.

"It was a lucky kill," the former mobster told the Sheriff. He was charged with intent to kill but took a plea bargin to help them bag the real killer. He would serve less than a year but that was certainly enough to preserve the Houghton name and legacy. All of Mississippi was pleased with that, particularly Governor Alverson.

He went on to explain that he had just finished cleaning in the kitchen after dinner and was actually planning to shoot Houghton the next day. All the other staff was gone. As he was leaving, he looked back and saw Jorge go in the back door toting a water can. Big Dog had only walked about fifty yards when he realized he had left his bag with his disguise in it. He slipped back into the kitchen, unnoticed, to get the bag from the pantry. That's when Houghton came in to get a snack.

He was so intoxicated that he could barely stand. Big Dog, hiding in the pantry, had a perfect view of what happened next. While Jorge watered the kitchen plants, he got a lucky break. He opened the basement door, and knowing it was only a matter of waiting before Houghton stumbled past, Jorge was there to give Houghton a deadly shove.

Of course, seeing what had happened, Big Dog was smart enough to get out of the kitchen when Jorge went down the stairs. He left the house immediately but hid out through the night, then dressed as a woman, took the first ferry out the next morning.

"And while it was a lucky break for us that the Georgia patrol pulled him over for speeding," commented Pepper, "the real hero—the real *heroine*—in this story is Stella Bankwell. It never occurred to me that pigeons were being used to bring messages to the island. She figured that out." With that, everyone at the table clapped and cheered... and Chatty who, of course, was sitting beside Stella, hugged her tight.

"I am so proud of my Stellie," he beamed.

Then, the Governor, at the head of the table, dabbed at the corner of his mouth with the cloth napkin and said, "I have a surprise. There's an unsung hero at this table."

"I though everyone had been sung—and one somebody even had many, too many, refrains," said Pepper, glancing at Chatty who frowned at him.

"In all that's happened, does anyone remember the good Sheriff here getting a call from Atlanta's top defense attorney?"

"I'd forgotten that!" Stella exclaimed. "I never thought about it again."

The Governor nodded, saying, "As had I, forgotten, Stella, until I received a call from that attorney, Jerry Hastings, this afternoon. He has a $50,000 retainer in the form of a cashier's check that he needs to return. He didn't have a phone number or mailing address." The Governor stopped for a moment and looked around the table. "So, Chatty, I told him that I'd have you call him first thing in the morning about getting back the money you'd put down assuring the best attorney for young Mr. Puckett."

"What?!" Stella practically screamed as excited talk started around the table welled up and Chatty's face reddened more than a little. "Oh, Chatty! You listened to me. You used your money to help someone else."

Pepper, who had been resenting Chatty all evening, suddenly had a wealth of admiration for him. "You were planning to pay for this big defense lawyer to represent Campbell and yet you hadn't said a word? That isn't like you."

Chatty comically rolled his eyes. "I know. I must be losing my touch."

They all laughed and Chatty's biggest reward was a hug from Stella. Campbell got up from his chair and came over to shake his hand and to hug him, too.

With his voice breaking, Campbell, in a crisp, beige-checked shirt, stood for a moment and explained how scary it had been to be railroaded. But to have so many people helping him was an unexpected show of kindnesses.

"I will do my best to repay each kindness from each person and add to it. Thank you all, so much."

The Governor stood with a crystal wine glass in his hand. "There are several heroes in this story. My wonderful Miss Alva who put up the bail money." He leaned over and kissed her on the cheek and she, as one might expect, blushed. "The great law enforcement agencies in this state, particularly my old friend, Sheriff Goudelock. No mystery is safe when Pepper and Stella are around, of course, with Chatty always trailing behind." That remark brought a laugh.

"Chatham, you outdid yourself this time and, most importantly, you told no one. I'm proud of you. And having known your father well, I can speak for him, too. His buttons would be popping with pride for you." Chatty wiped his eyes using a napkin. "There's a lot of good people at this table and a lot of good work has been done. But, Joseph Maycomb, this toast is to you. Your steadfast belief it was a murder is why Spencer Houghton got the justice he deserved. Let us raise a toast to you, young man."

As the table gave him a standing ovation, Joseph, who was typically shy, said, "Thank you. I'm going home to Sparta, tomorrow, for a few days because I want to tell my Grandpaw all about this. It will mean so much to him."

When dinner ended, and as people were leaving, Pepper finally saw his chance. Grabbing Stella's hand, he whispered, "C'mon out to the terrace."

Stella smiled and nodded as they, holding hands, hurried out, onto the terrace, where they were greeted by an

261

enormous full moon and a sky so full of stars, they almost seemed to be touching one another.

"Fitting, huh?" Pepper asked.

Stella was puzzled. "What's that?"

He put his arm around her. "A sky full of stars after dining at a table full of stars."

Stella giggled. And they shared a moment as Stella, waited, knowing she was about to be kissed. Pepper pushed back a wisp of her golden-red hair and just as he leaned in, Chatty came hurrying out the door.

"The Governor needs to talk to y'all. It has to do with something that's happened on Cumberland Island."

And just like that, the stars fell from the sky.

Acknowledgments

First, and foremost, my appreciation goes to Valerie Hepburn and Pat Hodnett Cooper who, knowing that Sapelo Island would be the second in a series of Stella Bankwell Mysteries, introduced me to a good man—and a great Southern character—who knows the island like the back of his hand. Without his help, I would have missed a lot of wonderful things about Sapelo.

I can't tell you his name because, almost immediately after he picked up my husband, Tink, and me at the ferry, he pointed his finger at me and said, "There's only one condition: I want no credit. Don't ever mention my name."

It's possible that he's in Witness Protection. Just kidding. He's a humble man who doesn't need accolades or attention, a rare find these days. He and his wife fed us, they loaned us a wonderful cottage, and he showed us every inch of the island; two different times, they had to put up with us but they did it with joy and good humor.

Cade Harp, the Executive Director of the Reynolds mansion, could not have been more gracious. He personally toured me through the mansion and explained so much. Georgia's Department of Natural Resources takes great pride in that island which the state bought from the widow of R.J. Reynolds, Jr. upon his death in 1964. The University of Georgia studies wild and marine life on the island and contributes to the world's knowledge of those species. They were all happy to help in any way possible. Judy Sartain provided legal advice on a couple of questions and proved, once again, what a good friend she is.

Stacy Rowe at the Visitors Center for the island, has become a cherished friend. He made the mistake of giving me his cell phone number. There were a few nights I had to call with questions. His knowledge is amazing and he has worked at the Visitors Center for twenty years so he knows it well.

John Tinker, my husband, took notes while we were on the island and, on the days when I felt I was out of words, he encouraged me and pushed me on.

Marc Jolley at Mercer University Press is always kind and is the only editor I've ever had who said, "Make these changes if you want but you don't have to." It was his smart idea to add a prologue to the book. It made a significant difference.

Though Allen Wallace has retired from Mercer, I will always be grateful that he discovered that I had the first Stella Bankwell book, then called Marc and they bought it within twenty-four hours.

Thank you to everyone else at Mercer whose hands touched this book. Particularly, I am grateful to the design team for a gorgeous cover and Mary Beth Kosowski who tweaked the cover. I thought it was wonderful before but Mary Beth perfected it. Kelly Land, Jenny Toole, and Marsha Luttrell also touched this book. Kelly's cheerfulness has made her a favorite with those who call Mercer University Press and hear her happy voice.

To booksellers, especially independents, thank you for supporting me all these years.

The enticing, adorable character of Chatham Balsam Colquitt IV was inspired by my beloved Edward Armstrong. I have said it's an over-the-top version of Edward but some of his friends say, "It's not over-the-top, it's Edward exactly." Tink and I have even taken to calling Edward "Chatty" because Chatty feels so real and so Edward to us."

Also, on St. Simons, I want to thank my longtime friend, Bess Thompson, Kelly and Robbie Ross, Luke Hodnett, as well as Elizabeth and Dick Pipe. They are filled with history and I learn so much from them. Though they are now in heaven, I will always be grateful to two of the most remarkable people I ever met: Roy and Anne Hodnett. They introduced me to the beautiful side of St. Simons. They never saw anything negative about the island even when hurricanes came and caused chaos.

Buff Leavy, the Publisher of the *Brunswick News*, doesn't know this but he gave me the idea for the first book about the St. Simons. I can't explain exactly why but at dinner one night, Edward was expressing his admiration for Buff and, as he talked, the idea began to plant itself. So, there! I owe Edward again.

If you haven't read the first in this series, please, don't miss *St. Simons Island: A Stella Bankwell Mystery.*

Parra Vaughn and her team at the Cloister always give me the opportunity to kick off each new Stella Bankwell book at that beautiful hotel. When you read this book, you will find incredible facts that link the Cloister and Sea Island to Sapelo. All the historical pieces in this book are true. I couldn't make up anything better than these bits and pieces.

It is not an exaggeration to say a divine force wrote this book. Thank you to everyone who prayed while I wrote, particularly Becky and Sonya Isaacs who got on the phone and prayed over me before I even started. My husband, my family, and my dear friend, Karen Peck prayed me on. One day, I was stuck and in despair. I called Karen's mother and she prayed the mightiest prayer over me. It worked because, by the next day, words were flying from my fingers.

From one of my dearest friends, Richard Childress, I learned the power of encouragement. When I was just out of college and working with a stock car race team, Childress observed my work ethic. One day he said, "You're a winner. You're going to have big achievements. Just wait and see." For many years, he encouraged me, this man who is successful in racing, vineyards, and even raising prize-winning cattle. These days, and for the last fifteen years, he calls to say, "I'm so proud of you. But I always knew you'd go far because you have spunk, smarts, and work so hard." Childress's example reminds me to encourage anyone I meet who has a dream. I ask you to please follow his example and lift people up with words of kindness and hope. It has really fueled me to find my dreams and to, eventually, create characters like Stella Bankwell and all her colorful, fun friends.

I am incredibly grateful to my Lord and Savior for giving me my childhood dream of writing books, which I have done now for twenty-five years. Also, to the almost fifty newspapers that carry my weekly column about life in the South, I am humbled by the grace and graciousness.

And to you, dear readers, thank you for reading this book and my others. It is because of you that I can carry on.

God bless you all.

The Author

Ronda Rich, whose Georgia family roots were planted around 1750, is the best-selling author of several books including *What Southern Women Know (That Every Woman Should)* and *The Town That Came A-Courtin'*, also a television movie. Her weekly syndicated column about Southern life appears in forty-seven newspapers across the Southeast.

Sapelo Island is her second Stella Bankwell mystery. *Saint Simons Island* was published in 2023. *Cumberland Island* is the next mystery, but first, there may be a Christmas surprise.

Learn more about her at www.rondarich.com.